THE PATH OF ASCENSION

VOLUME 1

WRITTEN BY
C. MANTIS

ART BY
KARLA DÍAZ

AETHON
BOOKS

vault

VOLUME 1

WRITTEN BY
C. MANTIS

ART BY
KARLA DÍAZ

AETHON BOOKS

vault

EDITORIAL
ADRIAN WASSEL — CCO & EDITOR-IN-CHIEF
DER-SHING HELMER — MANAGING EDITOR

DESIGN & PRODUCTION
TIM DANIEL — EVP, DESIGN & PRODUCTION
ADAM CAHOON — SENIOR DESIGNER & PRODUCTION ASSOCIATE
NATHAN GOODEN — CO-FOUNDER & SENIOR ARTIST

SALES & MARKETING
DAVID DISSANAYAKE — VP, SALES & MARKETING
SYNDEE BARWICK — DIRECTOR, BOOK MARKET SALES
BRITTA BUESCHER — DIRECTOR, SOCIAL MEDIA

OPERATIONS & STRATEGY
DAMIAN WASSEL — CEO & PUBLISHER
CHRIS KANALEY — CSO
F.J. DESANTO — HEAD OF FILM & TV

THE PATH OF ASCENSION, VOLUME 1, APRIL, 2025 COPYRIGHT © 2025, C MANTIS. ALL RIGHTS RESERVED. "THE PATH OF ASCENSION," THE PATH OF ASCENSION LOGO, AND THE LIKENESSES OF ALL CHARACTERS HEREIN ARE TRADEMARKS OF C MANTIS, UNLESS OTHERWISE NOTED. "VAULT" AND THE VAULT LOGO ARE TRADEMARKS OF VAULT STORYWORKS LLC. "AETHON BOOKS" AND THE AETHON BOOKS LOGO ARE TRADEMARKS OF AETHON BOOKS, LLC. NO PART OF THIS WORK MAY BE REPRODUCED, TRANSMITTED, STORED OR USED IN ANY FORM OR BY ANY MEANS GRAPHIC, ELECTRONIC, OR MECHANICAL, INCLUDING BUT NOT LIMITED TO PHOTOCOPYING, RECORDING, SCANNING, DIGITIZING, TAPING, WEB DISTRIBUTION, INFORMATION NETWORKS, OR INFORMATION STORAGE AND RETRIEVAL SYSTEMS, EXCEPT AS PERMITTED UNDER SECTION 107 OR 108 OF THE 1976 UNITED STATES COPYRIGHT ACT, WITHOUT THE PRIOR WRITTEN PERMISSION OF THE PUBLISHER. ALL NAMES, CHARACTERS, EVENTS, AND LOCALES IN THIS PUBLICATION ARE ENTIRELY FICTIONAL. ANY RESEMBLANCE TO ACTUAL PERSONS (LIVING OR DEAD), EVENTS, INSTITUTIONS, OR PLACES, WITHOUT SATIRIC INTENT, IS COINCIDENTAL. PRINTED IN USA. FOR INFORMATION ABOUT FOREIGN OR MULTIMEDIA RIGHTS, CONTACT: RIGHTS@VAULTCOMICS.COM

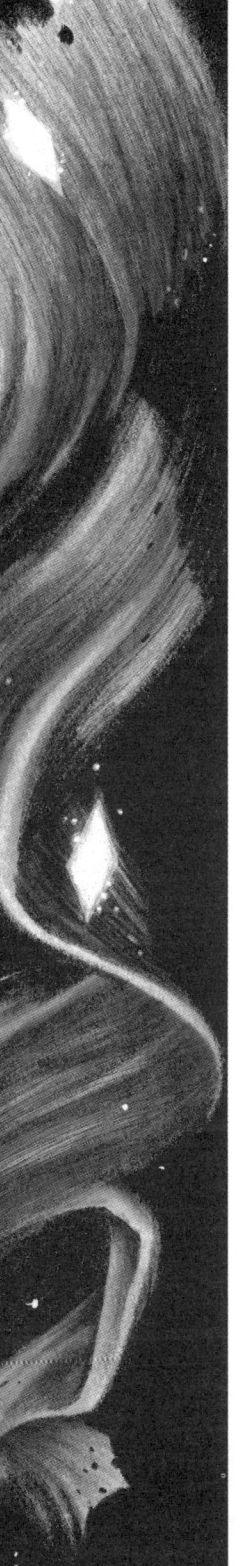

TABLE OF CONTENTS

Chapter 1	1
Chapter 2	17
Chapter 3	41
Chapter 4	65
Chapter 5	89
Chapter 6	115
Chapter 7	143
Chapter 8	169
Chapter 9	193
Chapter 10	221

Chapter 1

Matt looked at the result blinking on the screen in front of him. It was unbelievable, unacceptable.
Unchangeable.
He had done everything right. Followed every instruction. Pushed himself until the instructors forced him to rest. When his group of orphans turned nine, and the physical conditioning and rift-training tests began, he never slacked off or skipped lessons.

The one hundred and eighty-seven children of Warrington's Upper East Side Orphanage #3 had trained hard for their Awakening. Every profession was covered, and every combat role was touched upon. Even the more obscure variations were at least mentioned, if not directly trained for.

Matt could answer any question about any role or their sub-variations. He had studied every extra book his instructor's thought might be the slightest bit useful. Unwilling to be unprepared for a Talent that could change

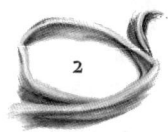

his weapon of choice, he practiced with every weapon the training armory had.

He preferred a longsword but was familiar with one-handed and shield combinations, dual-wielding daggers, weighted gloves, staffs, and even had practice time with the fake wands that simulated casting spells.

Matt was ready no matter what uses his Tier 1 Talent had.

However, Matt had not prepared for his Tier 1 Talent to be useless. Or worse than useless. He had not prepared for his Talent to be so bad the Empire's AI would officially rate it as 'detrimental.' That was a death blow to any potential career with an established guild.

Matt sat in the testing chair, wires still connected to his arm. Staring at the display that doomed him.

> **Tier 1 Talent determined.**
> Mana Regeneration inversely proportional to current mana, directly proportional to Maximum Mana.
> **Secondary Effect**: Essence cannot be applied to mana cultivation. Mana Regeneration is decoupled from mana cultivation.
> **Tertiary Effect**: Anomaly detected...
> ...
> ...
> ...
> Anomaly processed.
> Maximum Mana is substantially below average levels.
> Additional review required. Please, wait until a higher authority can be contacted.

Matt felt the blood drain from him. He was lightheaded, couldn't breathe. The screen blurred, words merging, sealing his fate with their little white proclamations.

Everything was falling apart and there was nothing he could d—

He focused on his primary effect! If that was good enough, then nothing else would matter. Heart pounding, Matt pulled up the complete description of the first aspect of his Talent.

He blinked when, in addition to the paragraphs he was expecting, a complicated mathematical formula and graph popped up. Apparently, the amount of mana he naturally regenerated varied dramatically depending on how full his pool was.

Matt froze when he noticed the percent signs on the graph. His Mana Regeneration was being measured as a percentage of his Maximum Mana. *He could generate mana at a rate equal to his Maximum Mana per second while below 1% of his total mana.*

What this meant was he could channel mana endlessly at an extremely high rate but any single use mana spells were effectively useless.

That was... insane. At low tiers, Mana Regeneration was usually so slow it was better measured in *mana per hour*. That was why mages dedicated massive amounts of their cultivation to improving their Mana Regeneration. Improving only the size of your pool and not how fast it filled led to mages constantly running out of mana.

Mages were forced to spend most of their cultivation on three separate, non-physical attributes from all the research he had done prior to his Awakening. This made them physically weaker and more vulnerable to

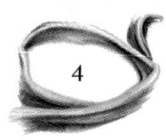

melee attacks, though many considered this a trade-off for the ability to summon fire out of nowhere. Matt certainly did.

Regenerating a percentage of his Maximum Mana meant Matt could completely sidestep this issue. By the time he dumped enough cultivation into his Maximum Mana to double the size of his mana pool, he would automatically have doubled the amount of mana he regenerated each second without spending anything on his Mana Regeneration.

Secondary Effect: Essence cannot be applied to mana cultivation.

Just like that, Matt's fantasy crumbled to pieces.

Before they raised tiers and began cultivating, people could typically hold only 100 mana in their pool, unless their Talent applied some boost to it. Conventional logic said the initial size of someone's mana pool barely mattered in the grand scheme of things. Even if Matt only started with 10 mana, by focusing a slightly heavier ratio into Maximum Mana, he could just stay at relatively low mana permanently while still casting endless spells. However, conventional logic assumed people could add essence into mana cultivation.

Matt looked back at his projected Mana Regeneration graph hopelessly. According to the AI, he would regenerate at a flat rate equivalent to his entire Maximum Mana per second for as long as his current mana was less than 1% of his maximum capacity.

Starting at zero mana, Matt needed only a fraction of a second to regenerate his pool to 1%. The instant he exceeded 1% of his Maximum Mana, though, his regeneration rate started plummeting below 1% of his capacity.

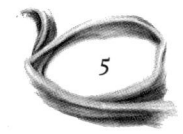

The AI even provided a little table showing how long it would take to reach certain benchmarks. It would take exactly ten minutes for Matt to reach 10% capacity but reaching 25% or 50% would take him months or years respectively.

While these rates were ludicrous, they were also irrelevant. With normal mages, getting to full capacity was important because it meant more spells to cast during a delve. In Matt's case, if he could raise his maximum up to 1,000 mana, then he'd regenerate 10 mana near instantaneously whenever he dropped under 10 mana. That was enough to endlessly cast a basic [Fireball] spell with a cost of exactly 10 mana.

No mage could cast any spell endlessly. Even if they had 100,000 mana, it would eventually be exhausted since normal Mana Regeneration was still calculated in mana per minute.

Secondary Effect: Essence cannot be applied to mana cultivation.

Those damning words shredded any hope Matt had still carried. Even melee fighters dedicated at least 30% of their essence to mana cultivation, just so they could use skills in battle. The most aggressive cultivation ratio he had heard of, from an actually successful rift delver at least, was 80% to physical and 20% to mana. And that was only possible because that particular delver's Tier 3 Talent let him negate the mana cost of skills based on his physical abilities.

Tier 3 Talent. That was his ticket out of this debacle. Matt never heard of a Talent set being purely detrimental. The ones that seemed useless at Tier 1 usually had synergy with that person's Tier 3 or Tier 25 Talents.

Matt could do thi—

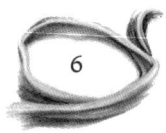

> *Higher authority reached.*
>
> ...
>
> *Anomaly resolved.*
>
> ...
>
> *Tertiary Effect: Lowered starting Maximum Mana.*
>
> *Maximum Mana determined to be 1.*

Matt felt as if he'd been punched in the gut yet again. A starting Maximum Mana less than what was needed to cast a [Fireball]. And he could never increase it. His stomach roiled with renewed vigor once the reality of his Tier 1 Talent's secondary effect set in again.

He stood out of the chair once the wires disconnected from his arm and the screen flashed and said, "Please, have a nice day," as if it was mocking him.

Looking around at the seemingly unfamiliar world, Matt tried to find anything or anyone that could fix him.

Everyone in here was an acquaintance he grew up with in the orphanage, no one who could turn back time. He had been with them since the mass rift breakout five years ago that destroyed half the city and orphaned so many kids like himself. As his gaze wandered, all the people he knew so well appeared alien to him.

They all looked so...happy.

A dozen feet away, Roxanne stood at a recruiter's desk for Victor's Elementals, a mage-focused guild that was the husband guild to Estor's Escalators, a physically oriented guild that acted to round out delve compositions so the parties were balanced.

Every word that came out of the recruiter's mouth made Roxanne smile more. The paperwork placed in front of her was quickly signed. She'd dreamed of being

a mage since their Introduction to Magic class all those years ago.

Matt wanted to feel happy for her, but nausea clawed at his stomach. He looked over to Gavle's Good Guilders, a respectable Tier 10 guild based on Ilstor, a neighboring Tier 12 planet. As he approached their booth, the head recruiter, Miles, stared at Matt with alarm.

"Ascender's balls, Matt! What's going on? I just got a notification saying your Talent isn't up to recruitment standards." Miles's head swiveled around, and he whispered, "Get over here." He reached out and snagged Matt's arm and pulled him into a vacant conference room behind the recruiting stands.

"What happened? I can't see the exact details, but your application was just booted back by our AI with..."

Miles held up the pad currently displaying Matt's conditional contract into GGG. He scrolled all the way down to show a flashing red box with the words 'applicant does not meet minimum requirements.'

"Is it *really* that bad?"

Matt debated what to tell Miles. He was a good guy who tried to get as many of the orphans into the fairly prestigious guild as he could. With Matt's knowledge and skill with a blade, Miles easily arranged a conditional contract for Matt with extremely good terms that only lasted ten years instead of the standard fifteen.

His percent-based mana regeneration could have been useful, if not for his pitiful Maximum Mana. So, he revealed the worst of it and ignored the solely useless parts.

"Completely unable to cultivate mana," Matt whispered. Venturing a glance over at Miles, the man had abruptly stopped pacing on the other side of the table.

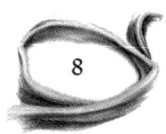

"Fuck.

"*Fuck*.

"**Fuck**."

Miles pressed his hands together in front of his face and started pacing again. Clearly deep in thought, he said, "There's not much I can do without getting both of us into trouble. If I show too much favoritism, other guilds might think I'm trying to create a spy to infiltrate another guild for us."

Matt waited and silently hoped Miles could think of a way for this not to be the end of his career as a delver.

Was he finished before he even started?

The nausea resurfaced even stronger than before, gnawing at him as the contents of his stomach fought to escape by any route necessary. With a deep breath and an effort of will, he forced his stomach to settle.

"I know that sounds like an excuse, but it's happened before. It would end in you getting blacklisted from any guild on this planet, and probably the neighboring ones, too. Even some of the city governments wouldn't allow you anywhere near them."

The next pause idled for what seemed like an eternity. "All right. The way I see it, you have two options. Well, only one viable option really. The other is a long shot at best.

"Best-case scenario, you somehow find a sponsor for The Path of Ascension. That would come with admission to the PlayPen Island. It's an Empire-run training facility only the best of the best get into."

Of course, Matt knew of The Path. It was literally legendary; the place where legends were forged, racing through the Tiers to become the heroes of the Empire.

As Matt opened his mouth to state he no longer fit that category, if he ever had, Miles held up a finger. "But there is a second way into the PlayPen. Most city adjuncts get a couple of slots per year to send promising youths. Getting one of those slots is even harder than usual in this city. The adjunct has been using them as political favors for the last ten years or so.

"That's the ideal case, but 99% of people never even sniff a PlayPen's air. More realistically, you need to buy a slot in a public Tier 1 rift. It's what freelance delvers do if there's too much competition for local rifts of their Tier."

He pulled his pad out and started tapping on it. "Ah. Here, in Glesie, two cities up the coast. They have a kobold Tier 1 rift, the going price is..."

Miles's eyes flicked around, scanning as he sucked in a breath. "Ten thousand credits. That's more than usual, but the price seems to have jumped in the last few years. That's the problem with a Tier 4 planet. At Tier 5, the planet would have far more Tier 1 rifts."

Miles spun the pad to show the listing that further confirmed his doom.

I'm fucked. It will take years to get that many credits. I'd be so far behind everyone else it would be terrible.

Matt forced himself to drop the self-pity and think about the situation more.

No, I don't care if I'm older than everyone at my Tier. I'll still become a delver and stop the rifts from overflowing again.

Earning ten thousand credits wouldn't be easy. That would take at least three years of work at any job willing to hire a thirteen-year-old. Let alone someone without a useful Tier 1 Talent and no job skills besides beginner delver training.

"Is there any chance I could join a lesser guild? Not that I don't want to join Gavle's, but it has to be easier to join a guild and get access to their rift than to get ten thousand credits, right?" Matt hoped for it to be true.

Miles's face hardened at Matt's question. He stared Matt right in the eyes and forcefully said, "Matt, with a Talent rating as bad as yours, it doesn't matter if your Tier 3 might fix the problem. No one here is going to willingly risk the resources to train you without a near illegal..." he grimaced, "or an actually illegal lifelong contract you'd never get out of. They'd take all your earnings or use some other nefarious deal to suck you dry."

Matt sputtered for a response, but Miles held up his hand and continued, "This planet is just too new and too poor. Just the teleportation to neighboring planets is too expensive for wasteful transits. Every inch of space is worth its weight in mana stones. A good 80% of the recruits we pick up today are never even going to leave this planet in the next five years. If they don't have clear potential, the Guild isn't going to shoulder that cost.

"Go ahead and try, but don't sign anything without reading the contract. Every single word. All recruitment contracts have to be in plain text that is easy to understand."

Miles reached into a cabinet along the wall and grabbed some cards. He held his hand out for Matt to shake and handed the cards over in his off-hand. "These are PlanetNet vouchers. Each card is good for an hour of uptime, and these five should get you through the next few years. The CityNet mostly just has general info, but the PlanetNet will let you check Glesie's rift status from time to time."

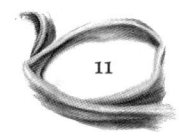

Miles looked drained all of the sudden. "Good luck, kid. And when you solo delve, play it safe and don't get injured. Healing will put you into crippling debt faster than anything else. Slow and methodical. Careful. Just be careful."

With that, Miles turned and trudged out of the room, and Matt took it as the dismissal it was.

He tried to help me, and his advice about the contracts is good to know. Without that warning, I might have jumped on the first offer without looking into it.

For the next hour, Matt traveled from stall to stall seeing if any guilds, corporations, or crafter associations would take a chance on him. But Miles had been right. Few were willing to even talk to him after seeing the detrimental rating for his Tier 1 Talent. Those who were still willing presented him with predatory lifelong contracts, all containing inescapable clauses where at least 50% of all his earnings were owed to the guild, even if he left the guild at some later point.

One particularly heinous contract had a line stating he forfeited ownership of his own body. Matt shuddered to think what people who accepted that contract ended up doing. Illegal prostitution would be the most preferable outcome, if the look the recruiter had given him was any indication.

Matt picked up the bag with his few belongings inside and headed for the door, eager to escape before he lost his breakfast all over the polished floor. The moment he got outside, he fertilized the shrubs next to the front entrance with the contents of his stomach.

After rinsing his mouth out, Matt stood up and headed away from the Awakening Center. He didn't know where he was going, but there was no point in standing around.

This being only a Tier 4 planet meant the resources needed to advance past Tier 3 weren't readily available for the population at large. The only reliable way to accumulate essence was to delve into the rifts and slay whatever monsters you found.

Some of the books Matt read referenced the air on the Empire's Tier 47 capital planet. The atmosphere alone held so much ambient essence people could cultivate without delving into rifts. On this backwater, the ambient essence was near zero.

Transportation off the planet is too expensive. No guild will accept me unless my Tier 3 Talent is synergistic enough with my Tier 1 and lets me accumulate more mana so I'm not crippled.

Or unless I sign my life away.

Matt pondered his next steps.

I need a job.

Thirteen wasn't *technically* considered an adult, at least not by the Empire's normal standards. Starting today, though, they were all on their own. The orphanage just didn't have the room or resources to spare on older children when most could find employment or an apprenticeship after receiving their Tier 1 Talents.

To relieve some of the crushing stress on the orphanages, both emancipation and Awakening were performed early on Lilly. Orphans were made legal adults at the age of thirteen instead of the usual late fourteen or fifteen when Awakening normally happened.

Matt wandered south. The further he walked, the more lingering damage he came across from the rift break five years ago.

While the debris was mostly cleaned up and repaired on the northern side of the city, the southern section still carried battle scars in the form of the occasional burned-out building still waiting to be demolished and rebuilt.

As Matt passed a crater where some great spell had ripped into the horde of monsters, rainwater filling in the bottom had turned it into a stagnant pool thick with algae growing on top.

Just another sign of what happened when rifts weren't delved regularly enough. Another bleak reminder of the loss of his parents and the destruction of his city.

When searching the CityNet as he wandered aimlessly, Matt found a business called Benny's Inn advertising an open position for 'general staff. No skills needed. Room and board included. Pays four hundred credits a month.'

The description was lacking in detail, worryingly so. But with that kind of pay, Matt at least had to try. It offered more than any of the other unskilled labor jobs being advertised.

Matt looked up directions and followed the road for several more miles until he came upon Benny's Inn. It was right near the edge of the five-mile coastline that served as the safe zone, the water preventing rifts from spawning.

Benny's Inn was situated on the trail leading to the closest Tier 4 rift in the region, the highest Tier available on the planet. It also had the benefit of being near the trailheads leading to the three Tier 3 rifts closest to the city. That made Benny's the best place for local parties and groups to relax and recuperate between delves.

They say delvers spend way more credits than normal cultivators, so I need to work near delving to reach Tier 3 anytime soon. To reach a city with a public Tier 1 rift, I need money. The ten thousand credits on their own won't be enough. At the very least, I'll also need to buy gear and cover travel money.

What Matt found at the end of the road was a six-story building with a large, garish sign proclaiming the owner's name.

When he opened the front door, Matt found a large common area with a bar at the center surrounded by tightly packed tables and seating. Behind the counter, a big man in a greasy apron gave only a quick glance to Matt in the open door before immediately returning to whatever he was doing behind the bar.

As Matt approached, the man gruffly barked out, "Kid, unless you're a paying customer, fuck right on off. No charity. No donations." He never even bothered to look back up.

Matt braced himself and gathered all the cheer he could muster despite the man's tone. "No, sir. I'm here to talk to Benny about the position that was posted. Can I assume that's you, sir?"

That got the fat man to look back up. He scanned Matt with squinted eyes before asking "Lemme guess. Shitty Tier 1, kid?"

Matt swallowed hard before answering with what dignity he could, "Yes, sir."

"Got any inkling what the job entails?"

"No, sir, but I'm willing to work hard. I'm—"

Benny cut him off. "Yeah, yeah. I already expect that, and I won't put up with nothin' less. What I need is a floater. Somebody who can do any job. Jump between 'em as needed."

Benny's eyes flicked around, and then back at Matt. "Might mean you scrub toilets. Might mean you help the girls carry out food when it's busy. Hours are from five in the morning to midnight, with a two-hour break 'round noon. You get four hundred credits a month, no tips. I see you take a tip, I kick your ass out."

Matt ground his teeth as much as he could without letting it show. The old bastard had him good. That kind of pay was excellent, even if it sounded like he'd be earning every credit.

The delve slot in Glesie was ten thousand credits, and that was his last lifeline. Simply too many people needed the low-tier rifts, and there were not enough of them to go around. Slots were bought, then later resold when the delvers team outgrew the rift's Tier, so credits wouldn't be wasted. Nonetheless, the barrier to entry was high.

A little more than two years. That's all. Call it two and a half for extra expenses. I can do this.

Matt's decision was already made.

"Where do you want me to start, sir?"

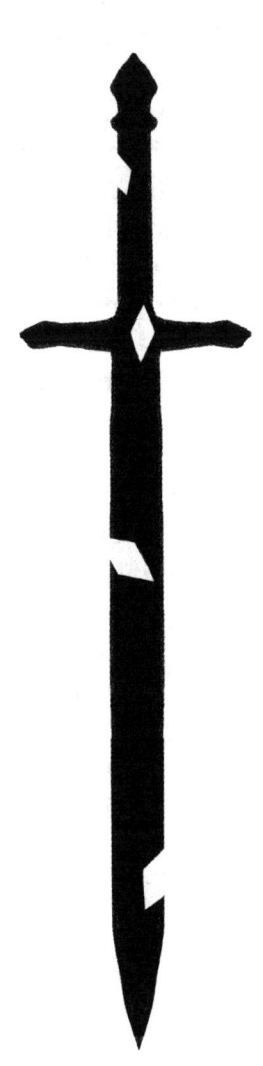

Chapter 2

"Matt, I need you to check the staff bathroom. The water is really slow," Beatrice called out as she passed by.

"Is it the hot, the cold, or both, Bee?" Matt shot back from the maintenance room, where he was assembling a table. He got no response. Apparently, Beatrice had already returned to the slow lunch crowd.

Matt decided to finish the table first. They needed it more. Last week, a bar fight had destroyed nearly half of the tables in the common room before it was brought under control.

The problem was, they had a limited number of spare tables in reserve. It'd been just enough to keep the common room from having *too many* gaps, but just barely. To make the room feel less empty, they had spread the remaining ones out, which only worked because they hadn't been slammed yet. But with the weekend approaching, they needed the seating. So, Matt had been

making tables in all his spare time to refill the common room, and then get their surplus back.

If Benny wasn't such a tight ass with money and just bought better tables instead of treating them as disposable, I wouldn't be playing amateur carpenter every other week. Or if he just hired a bouncer.

Matt finished the table and grabbed his plumbing bag. As he walked through the common room, he looked for Beatrice, but she was nowhere to be seen. He sighed. Of course, two customers were already at the bar, clearly waiting to be helped. Matt didn't recognize them, which meant they were probably new customers.

Where is Beatrice? Must be nice to be able to slip out for a dozen smoke breaks just because you sleep with the boss.

That made him pause. Maybe she did earn the extra breaks. After all, no one else wanted to be near the man longer than absolutely necessary.

If Matt didn't help the new customers, Benny would have his ass despite it being Beatrice's job to man the common area.

Matt hurried over to the front desk part of the bar and greeted the guests. "Hello! How can I help you this afternoon, sir and ma'am?" Benny expected unfailing politeness to his guests and would side with any paying customer over his staff on any issue.

The man answered, "We'd like a room, please. But we don't know how long we'll be in the area. So, what can you do for around, umm...say a two-week stay, with the option of it going longer?" As he leaned forward, Matt got a better look at him under the bar's brighter lighting.

He was tall. Based on Matt's 5'10", he was at least 6'2", possibly up to 6'4". Dark hair and gray eyes with a face that, while hard, looked used to laughing. The woman

next to him was probably 5'9". The ponytail of copper-colored hair made her green eyes pop even more in the dim lights in an almost disturbing contradiction to her classically attractive face.

What took Matt by surprise wasn't their good looks, it was that these two felt far stronger to his spiritual sense than the normal Tier 2s and Tier 3s that usually frequented Benny's Inn. Even stronger than the Tier 4s that came around, though that was beyond his ability to get a good sense of. He pegged them at the peak of Tier 4 or possibly even Tier 5.

It made Matt nervous. If these two wanted to start trouble, no one here could stop them. No one would even want to try.

Who knew what an enraged pair of Tier 5s could do? Matt didn't want to find out.

If they felt slighted, no one was there to greet them... I don't want to think about what Benny would do to me to keep in their good graces.

Being fired would be the least of his problems in that situation. Rumors still circulated about former employees who were never seen again. Supposedly just rumors, but Matt wasn't interested in testing their veracity.

"Yes, sir. We have several packages that might suit your needs. If you'd like, we can offer a room for a week and, after that, you can just pay by the day at about the same rate. It comes with unlimited access to the training room and three meals a day. It would all be for just four hundred credits the first week and then sixty credits a day going forward. Is that something you'd be interested in?"

The woman answered, "We'll take it. Can you show us to our room, please? Then to the training room." She swiped her hand at the payment reader, and Matt saw 'accepted' immediately appear.

That was a pleasant surprise. Despite Tier 1 mana stones being worth one hundred credits, the price was still enough that most people complained and tried to haggle.

"Yes, ma'am." Matt did as requested.

The duo only stayed in their room long enough to drop off their bags. Then Matt led them to the training room, where the woman looked around at the training dummies in obvious disappointment.

Why is she disappointed? The training aids are only years old and updated with the newest software for attack and defense patterns of Tier 4 speed. It's one of the few actually nice things this place has.

"Is there something wrong, ma'am? The training aids go up to Tier 4, and the software was just upd—"

Before Matt could finish, she waved him off and sighed. "No, it's fine. I just forgot where we were for a moment." Her flashed smile took the sting out of the comment.

Matt decided to leave before she could take her obvious disappointment out on him. He had a sink to fix anyway.

Just one more year. Keep your chin up. You got this.

The alarm started blaring at 3:55 a.m., and Matt was down at the training room by 4:00 a.m. He could squeeze in two hours of practice time before Benny was up and assigned him tasks.

Matt started with a few warmup stretches, then used the variable weight bar to do strength training. Today was legs, which meant he would be walking like a newborn until tomorrow, but Matt had to admit he liked the tingle.

Using part of the PlanetNet vouchers Miles had given him, he had long ago found a training routine good for a young man looking to be a melee delver. It wasn't amazing, but it was free and didn't require proprietary supplements or a subscription to a sketchy netsite like so many others did.

As he completed each set, he recorded his weights and sets while trying to keep the fatigue at bay. For the last year, he'd put in as much physical training as he could manage while still needing to work twelve-hour days. While he had clear results to show for it, he was perpetually bone tired. Even when he slept, he felt tired.

Each rep was paired with the mantra, '*One more year.*' When the time came, he had to be ready to delve a rift with only his physical abilities.

After weight training, Matt took his usual practice-longsword down and started a Tier 2 combat sequence on the training dummy. It was faster and stronger than him at this setting and, with his wobbly legs, his ever-rotating collection of bruises would grow again.

Matt practiced in rounds of five minutes, trying to inflict damage while avoiding being hit as much as possible. Everything he read on the CityNet said injuries were what retired most low Tiered delvers.

With few Healers on the planet and fewer still who had their skill as public knowledge, most injuries could only be healed with mundane methods. That meant months of recovery if it was serious. Which meant months of not delving and not progressing. It meant months of wasted income and increased debt.

I can't afford to get injured. Literally.

This sucks. Living on a low Tiered planet means anyone with a healing Talent or an innate healing skill immediately gets snatched up by the guilds and shipped off planet. It leaves only the lucky few who get a healing skill as a rift reward and don't take that opportunity to join a guild and do the same. Or the few idiots insane enough to sell such a valuable skill shard.

Can I blame them for bailing, though? I was going to do the same. Am I just bitter I couldn't escape this backwater shithole?

Matt had to admit that sounded truer than he'd like.

The training aid landed a blow that brought Matt out of contemplation and back into the fight. With a pivot and an upward slash, Matt deflected the next blow and brought his sword down on the training aid's collarbone. The blow was hard and clean enough that the lights flashed red, signifying a 'kill.'

The aid had a programming oversight that didn't handle overhead attacks on its right side well. It was hard not to abuse it. Matt didn't want to develop habits that might get him killed but finding an obvious flaw in an opponent was possible, too.

The *beep* chimed, signifying the start of his three-minute rest interval.

He picked up his water bottle, wiped the sweat off his face, and stretched. When he noticed someone was in the other corner of the room, he came to a halt.

Shit! Is it that late already? Am I late for work?

Matt quickly checked his pad and saw it was only 4:23 a.m. Looking closer, there were actually two someone's loitering in the corner, the man and woman who had checked in yesterday.

The strong ones.

He didn't want any trouble, so he turned down the volume on his pad so the beeps wouldn't disturb the training duo. The last thing he wanted to do was piss off a customer, let alone a powerhouse who could probably level the building in seconds. Matt wasn't sure what a Tier 5 was capable of, but he knew they were stronger than most people on the planet. Lilly was only a Tier 4 world and, therefore, only had rifts up to Tier 4. Anyone higher Tier than that needed to travel off-world to find higher Tier rifts to help them progress.

Matt continued to practice in intervals. As a Tier 1, he didn't have enough essence or physical cultivation to keep up with nonstop, high-intensity combat. Right now, he was only marginally stronger than he'd been before his Awakening.

During a lesson about high Tier cultivators at the orphanage, he had seen a recording of a competition between two Tier 15 participants. The combatants were so evenly matched the fight lasted over an hour of nonstop fighting. Matt's heart would explode if he fought at that intensity for that long.

Cultivation was the journey of power and strength, after all. The normal human limitations quickly fell away as you ascended.

Matt cleaned up his area and stored the training aid along the wall, preparing to go shower. As he crossed the common room toward the staff housing hall, he saw Zephyr. The old man had first stumbled in around two months ago and never quite stumbled back out. The entire time he'd been here, Zephyr followed a strict routine; he drank until he passed out on a table, woke up, and then kept drinking.

Matt had eventually taken it upon himself to make sure the grumpy old bastard got into his bed most nights and ate at least one meal a day. The look of loss and despair in the man's eyes was easy to recognize.

It stared back at him every time he looked in a mirror.

He saw it in everyone who'd lost people in the rift breaks.

He couldn't fix Zephyr, but he could at least stop him from killing himself before he worked past whatever loss had broken him.

"Come on, Zephyr. You need to sleep. Preferably in a bed. And drink this." Matt shoved his water bottle in the man's hand and glared till he finished it off.

"All right, give me your arm." He hooked an arm under Zephyr's and helped the man shuffle to his room. He grumbled nonsense at Matt the whole time.

A Tier 4 reduced to this is just depressing. Who did he lose to end up like this? Spouse? Kid? Mother? Father? Brother? Sister? Some shitty combination of those?

Matt fished the key card out of Zephyr's pocket and dumped the old man on his bed. Before he left, he filled a glass with water and left it on the nightstand.

Is there really no escaping the pain? Will ascending to higher Tiers not even help?

The next morning, Matt once again started in the training room. At 5:00 a.m., the redhead and the dark-haired man strolled in. Unlike yesterday, though, the redhead came over to his side of the gym. Once she confirmed she had his attention, the woman held out a hand to shake.

"The name's Dena. Sorry, I either didn't get your name when we checked in or forgot," she said with a smile that removed any sting from her forgetting his name.

"No, ma'am. That's my bad. I must not have introduced myself. The name is Matt." He took her hand and gave it a firm shake. "Is there something I can help with, ma'am?"

"There actually is. I'm in need of a sparring partner who specializes in longswords. My husband Eric, over there..." She pointed a thumb over her shoulder at the man, who just nodded along at the mention of his name. His concentration was fully aimed at a floating ball circling his hand. "He's too busy working on his mana control. Would you be interested? I'd pay the standard fee."

Matt *was* interested, but there was no way he could take Dena's money. If Benny found out, he'd be out on his ass so quick his head would spin. Then he'd be truly screwed.

"I'd be happy to help, ma'am. Though I can't accept any payment. Part of my duties is to assist guests in any way I can."

Dena gave him a look that said she sensed something was wrong but wasn't going to press it.

"How would you like to spar, ma'am? I'm only a Tier 1, so I won't be able to challenge you. But if you need to practice a certain move or technique, I'm happy to fill whatever role you need me to."

"I'm more looking to practice my staff technique against the longer weapon, so I'll reduce my speed and strength to match yours."

Matt shrugged. "Whenever you're ready, ma'am."

He pulled his longsword up into a neutral stance. When Dena moved, Matt sidestepped the thrusting butt of her staff and retaliated with a cut toward her leg, but she stepped out of range of the slash.

As the fight progressed, it became clear Dena wasn't very used to the staff. Which was probably the only thing that stopped her from easily annihilating him. Even with her speed and strength reduced to near his levels, Matt struggled to take the lead.

Whatever her normal weapons were, she was well accustomed to melee fighting, and it showed. The Tier 5 was always ready for every move he could think of, and it let her control the flow of the fight effortlessly.

She called the end of the spars at 6:00 a.m. after several rounds of combat. The breaks in between were purely for Matt's benefit. Even after an hour of training, she'd yet to sweat a single drop.

Reaching a higher Tier truly was stepping above the common man.

"Do you train here every day? Or do you have a set schedule? This was a far better practice than I thought it would be. You have good instincts with that longsword of yours."

Matt futilely tried to get his breathing under control before answering, "I'm here every morning, ma'am. Also, I'd be happy to spar with you as much as you'd like. It was far better than the training dummies even turned up to Tier 2."

"Good. I'll see you tomorrow, then."

Every morning for the next month and a half, Matt sparred with Dena. Occasionally, Eric would get fed up with his mana control exercises and also treat him to a thrilling longsword vs. longsword sparring match.

Apparently, the taller man was the dedicated melee fighter of the duo, but he'd found his mana control to be lacking recently and worked to shore that up.

The few suggestions Eric gave Matt about longsword combat had greatly increased his confidence with the blade. The advice was nothing revolutionary, but he shared tips about attacking from unexpected angles and a few feints that Matt found enlightening. Matt believed he was good, but the older man seemed to be one with the sword.

Surprisingly, Eric preferred an ax but said no melee fighter could rely on just one weapon. You had to be at least proficient with most of them. Monsters came in infinite variations. Some would eventually be resistant to or problematic to fight with your preferred weapon type.

Those were probably the best weeks of Matt's life. Dena and Eric were nice to him, didn't treat him like spare luggage they were trying to get rid of or as a charity case because his parents were dead.

The couple gave him respect, even though they were so much stronger than him. They could have treated him like something you'd scrape off a shoe and no one would have looked askance at them for it. He'd received invitations to eat with them a few times, and even Benny hadn't said anything during the occasional meal.

Matt swore to himself that when he was that strong, he would remember their kindness and strive to show the same to others. So many of the delvers coming through Benny's treated anyone weaker than them as sub-human and fawned over anyone stronger. It was all so fake. So meaningless. He wanted nothing to do with it.

"Hey, Matt. You don't have to answer if you don't want to, but I've got to ask. Why are you here?" Dena looked awkward as she asked. Even Eric looked up from his mana control trainer, which he put away to stand and join the conversation.

"You're strong, good with a blade, and very hard-working. I'm just confused as to why you haven't been snatched up by a guild or party already?"

Matt sighed. "No real secret to it. My Tier 1 Talent doesn't allow for any mana cultivation. That invalidated my contract with the guild I was going to join. Any other guilds willing to take me had terms so absurd I might as well have sold myself into slavery."

Dena winced, and Eric mirrored her expression. She opened her mouth to speak, clearly going to apologize for something that wasn't her fault. So, Matt cut her off. He didn't want their pity.

"That's why I'm working here. Miles, the head guild representative, did what he could to help me. He wasn't able to do much, but he pointed me in the direction I needed to go. That's why I'm here, saving up money to purchase a slot in a Tier 1 dungeon. Everyone says there are no purely detrimental Talents, just paired talents you need to advance to fix. So, I'll be a solo delver and advance on my own. It's not even a purely bad thing, delving solo. I won't have to share the essence, so I'll advance faster, which will let me catch up with my age group.

"Hopefully, the problem is solved at Tier 3 and not Tier 25." Matt tried to lighten the atmosphere with a joke, but the pair just stared at him for a long moment.

"Well, that's a shit hand to get dealt. But you didn't give up, which is the most important part. If this planet were a higher Tier, you'd be picked up by a guild for that alone. So many delvers lose the will to continue, the drive to advance. And that's not something a Talent can compensate for." Eric shook his head.

On that sour note, Matt went about his day, resolved to avoid thinking about his Talent more than he had to.

That night, another big fight broke out; one worse than the usual two-to-six-person brawl.

The party of delvers responsible for starting it came in later than most, so the common area was already crowded with parties eating and drinking. They sauntered in as

if they'd just found the crown jewels of the Emperor himself.

Their attitude attracted everyone as they walked to the item identifier. Without hesitation, their leader walked up to the man about to use it and shoved him out of the way violently.

The air of anticipation built as they placed a skill shard in the reader. Skill shards were a rare drop at this planet's Tier, but they could vary in usefulness. This group was so cocky and sure they got a good skill, they didn't even bother to set the readout to be sent privately to their pads. Instead, the process was displayed on the large screen for the whole crowd to see.

The reason for their arrogance was readily apparent when the first lines of text appeared.

> *Analyzing skill shard...*
> *Cracked skill shard detected. Requesting a higher authority to complete analysis.*

A cracked skill shard was a rare variation of shard modified off the baseline. The change could be anything and finding two that were identical was said to be impossible.

The most famous cracked skill Matt knew of was a cracked version of [Shadow Sword]. The original skill projected a copy of the weapon to the side during a strike. Nothing crazy. The 'shadow' was only a quarter the strength of the original strike, making it useful but not amazing.

The infamous cracked version allowed the user to summon fully autonomous shadow swords. This was superior to even comparable skills like [Sword Minion] and [Sword Doppelganger]. The former needed real blades and the user's concentration to control them. The latter was just a single sword that, while autonomous and equal in strength to the original, lacked durability and could be shattered with a powerful enough hit.

That [Cracked Shadow Sword] let the user summon *endless* autonomous copies at only a quarter strength. Having hundreds of blades that worked together in perfect harmony made it a skill everyone feared.

Matt blanked on the name of the individual who had gotten the skill but could remember they'd carved themselves out an earldom spanning several new planets with that skill alone.

Are we going to see the birth of a legend here?

Matt hoped not. Desperately.

If the cracked skill turned out to be a useful variation and not neutral or detrimental, this night would turn into a bloodbath. These idiots should have never revealed it publicly. They could get themselves and, more importantly, Matt, killed in the rush to steal the skill.

Just as Matt moved to escape the crowd on the cusp of exploding, the man who'd been holding the skill, and who was probably the party leader, got everyone's attention. Still with his back to the crowd, in a voice dripping with arrogance, he called out, "I'd love to meet the people stupid enough to attack the son of Brackus of Brackus Holdings."

That's what he's relying on to keep him safe?

Matt was flabbergasted. Brackus Holdings was a local courier service. While they had some influence and power, they weren't nearly enough of a deterrent to stop

people from killing his arrogant ass. The only difference was now they'd make sure to kill all the witnesses, too.

He spun, intent on slipping out, but saw Zephyr passed out on a table not too far from the item identifier. For a moment, Matt debated leaving the old man to his fate. It was his own fault he'd chosen a spot right where the action would be fiercest.

Just leave him. Getting yourself killed to save a drunk isn't worth it. Just go.

Matt cursed at himself even as he started toward the old man. In the end, he couldn't just stand by. Inaction was a choice; one he refused to make.

The trick would be getting close without attracting attention or triggering a stampede toward the party at the item identifier.

The item identifier beeped right as Matt slid up to Zephyr's table.

The noise grabbed everyone's attention, including his.

Analysis complete...
Skill shard identified as [Cracked Phantom Armor].

Original Skill Description: Tier 14 skill. Pre-charge 200 or more mana into the skill. When a lethal blow is detected, skill will automatically activate and block the attack. Alternatively, skill can be activated at the user's discretion.

Cracked Skill Description: Channel mana into the skill to activate [Phantom Armor], which will then block physical and elemental

damage with efficiency depending on the rate at which mana is channeled into the skill.

<u>Rating:</u> **Detrimental** - Extremely niche or limited use due to mana cost being continuous. Crack turns a highly sought-after, life-saving skill into a costly and inefficient general defense skill. Possibly recommended for mages with a strong emphasis on Mana Regeneration cultivation.

Matt swallowed. No one would be getting murdered for *that* skill shard. However, judging by the look on the party leader's face and the crowd's growing laughter, a brawl was about to break out anyway.

Matt hoisted Zephyr up and whispered, "Start moving. We need to move. Now."

Before he could get Zephyr balanced on his wobbly legs, the man who had been pushed aside earlier spat at the party. "Hah! That's what you arrogant pricks get for cutting—"

Before he could finish, the son of Brackus of Brackus Holdings snatched the skill shard out of the reader and hurled it at the man. While he ducked to the side of the projectile, his attacker took that opportunity to bash him in the face. With the first punch thrown, both parties went at it, and it immediately spread to the rest of the room.

People took the opportunity to get aggression out or settle grudges.

Matt pulled Zephyr along, no longer trying to be subtle and just trying to find the edge of the fighting. He didn't want to get crippled by an errant blow from

someone multiple Tiers above him. Benny wouldn't cover the cost of healing him after all.

They had almost made it when something hit him from behind. As he and Zephyr tumbled to the ground, Matt picked out a gleam under a broken chair leg.

It was the skill shard.

Matt's world slowed.

He glanced at Zephyr and saw the man was completely out of it, eyes closed, mouth slack.

I have to take the chance. It may be useless for most, but I could use it. I just hope this doesn't get me killed.

Matt quickly grabbed the chair leg, and the skill shard with it. As he pulled Zephyr back to his feet, he raised the chair leg threateningly while letting the skill shard slip into his sleeve.

Carefully, he swung the chair leg at someone's back and let that knock the wooden weapon out of his hands. Then he switched the arm he held Zephyr with, trapping the skill shard in his elbow.

The feeling of the small crystal shard pressing into his flesh haunted Matt's every step and pumped adrenaline through his veins like never before.

Once he and Zephyr were out of the brawl, he carried the old drunk to his room, quickly dumping him on the bed before heading to the maintenance room. As Matt closed the door and ensured he couldn't possibly be seen by Zephyr, and before he fully stepped into the hallway in view of the cameras, he shoved his right hand into his pocket and let the skill shard slide down his sleeve and fall in.

His heart was racing, but not from the fight. He had been an unwilling participant in more than one of

them. No, it was the danger of the stolen skill causing him to spiral.

When Matt entered the maintenance room, he prepared to make tables and chairs as a cover. Benny popped in not five minutes later, once the noise died down a bit.

"Oh, good, you already started. And I saw you getting the old man out of there. I can't charge him rent if he's dead. So, good work."

Matt resisted the urge to scowl when Benny made callous statements like that. He had practice. The comments were commonplace.

"No problem, Boss. What's the damage? Do we need more tables or chairs?"

"Tables. People can eat standing up, but no one wants to eat on their lap. If they wanted to sit, they wouldn't use my chairs as fucking weapons." With that, Benny stomped out.

Matt let out the breath he'd been holding.

He'd almost shit himself when Benny said, 'I saw you.' Matt expected Benny to check on him, but if he had seen him steal the skill shard, Benny would have just killed him. Useful or not and lazy as he was, Benny still treated his customers like they were his only source of income. Which they were.

Matt knew he shouldn't be checked on for the rest of the night, and there were no cameras in the maintenance room. The spare tables and chairs were kept in a separate storage room, so there should be no interruptions while he hid the skill shard.

If the arrogant party complained the skill shard was missing, which Matt bet they would, Benny would try and appease them by searching the staff. It was Benny's

standard practice, so he could say he did his best, then do nothing else.

Matt grabbed a finished table and wedged it under the door handle. Then he went to the desk and pulled out his pad.

It was an older model that had seen numerous repairs by Matt and the previous owners. He pulled out a shim, carefully pried off the back, and immediately ripped out the speaker. The pad's sound system was subpar and intermittently went out, so it was no real loss.

In the newly opened space, Matt carefully placed the skill gem. It was a close fit. Thankfully, the shard was oblong, a little less than an inch long and a quarter inch wide in the middle.

He quickly inspected his work and guesstimated it would work. Most of the cramped internals were taken up by the screen. The processor was small, and the mana battery was even smaller. He had the skill shard nestled in next to the battery right where the speaker had been.

Matt grabbed a hot glue gun. After an eternity waiting for it to heat up, he applied a drop under the skill shard, stopping it from rattling and giving its hiding place away.

As fast as his shaking hands could move, he closed the pad back up and checked to make sure it still worked. Nothing seemed amiss. Matt shook it to see if he could hear anything move.

Not a sound. It was perfect.

After cleaning up and putting everything away, Matt smiled and was about to get back to making tables when he saw the small speaker. He couldn't leave it out. It wasn't like anyone else came in here, but leaving any clue to his theft was stupid, suicidally so.

He proceeded to smash the small speaker until only an indiscernible powder remained, which was tossed to intermingle with the dust and debris already in the shop.

With the evidence of his theft taken care of, Matt removed the table he used to bar the door against interruptions and began making new tables. After about an hour, the shouting started. Matt repressed a smile. Shortly after that, Benny came in with the irate party leader.

As soon as Brackus's idiot son saw Matt, he started screaming, "Did you steal it, boy?! I'll fucking kill you if you took it!"

Inside, Matt smiled. That was all he needed to hear. It was a question, not a statement.

Outwardly, Matt put on a surprised face and stood up. "Steal what, sir? I didn't steal anything. Benny would kill me if I did, and I've been working here for over a year. Never stole a thing."

The man didn't seem to care, but the show was for Benny not him. He had a wand in his hand he pointed at Matt.

Matt knew what it was, a mana detector. These things only worked at close ranges but would find Mana Concentrations. A skill shard would be detected if said skill shard wasn't right next to a mana battery, which would overpower any reading with unstructured mana. Even if he replaced the battery with the skill shard, so long as no one tried to mess with the pad, they wouldn't think anything was amiss but a broken pad.

Even if the wand picked something up. Mana was supposed to be there after all.

Matt hadn't expected the man to have a detector like this on hand, but it was a standard tool used at the orphanage to check for any kind of mana contraband. There was nothing to be concerned about. While he personally hadn't smuggled anything in, kids liked to brag about their successes, and the best smuggling methods were well-known by all the orphans.

This was a very reliable way to beat the scanners.

"C'mere, Matty. Let Mr. Brackus scan you. Doubt you took it but, if you did, say so now. Even if you swallowed the thing, the wand will find it. Don't do nothin' stupid," Benny recited through a bored expression, clearly only humoring the man.

With nothing to fear, Matt walked over and let the pompous ass run the wand over him, focusing on his stomach, shoes, and pockets. After a murmured curse, he waved the wand over all the drawers. When he repeatedly found nothing out of the ordinary, he stormed out.

Wanting to reinforce his alibi, he stopped Benny before he left. "Wouldn't it be more likely that someone else took it and absorbed it already?"

Benny yawned out, "Nah. Not that anyone would want to take that shit skill, but it takes days to absorb one." As he was leaving, he examined the tables Matt had stacked in a corner. "That's enough for tonight, just get some sleep and finish tomorrow. All this ruckus over a great life-saving skill turned into a shitty defensive one. Whoever heard of a channeled defensive skill? No one can afford that kind of mana cost."

As Benny turned the corner, Matt heard the murmuring turn to 'arrogant whelps who throw skill shards then want them back.'

Matt was surprised Benny didn't try and get him to stay up all night to finish. He had before. "Thanks, Boss. I'll be sure to finish it first thing tomorrow."

Not caring if Benny heard him, Matt took the excuse offered and fled to his room.

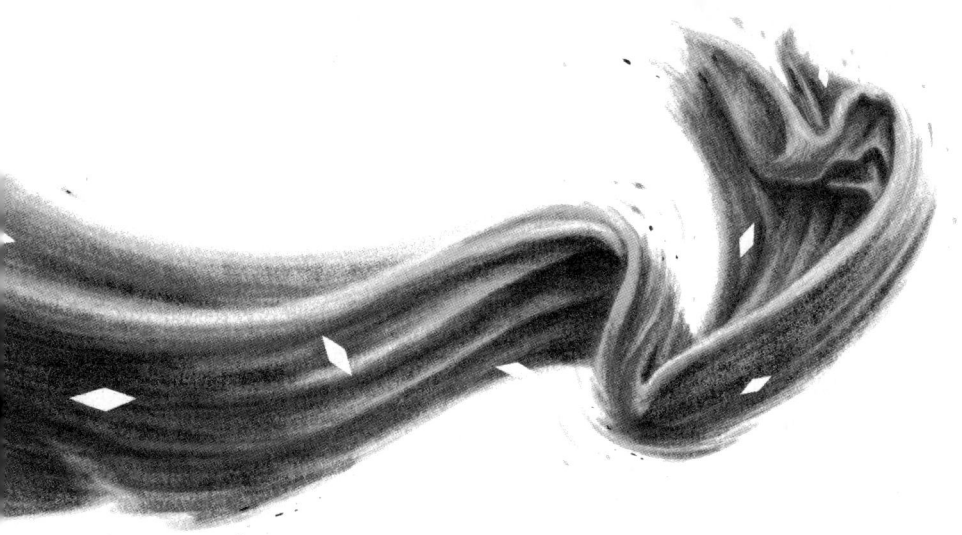

Chapter 3

Lying in the dark, Matt cradled the pad in his hands. He had tried to get some rest, but the anticipation and thrill of getting away with the theft kept sleep away.

He looked at his pad again. This was his lifeline. Some part of him kept expecting Benny or the party leader to burst into the room and snatch the pad and skill shard out of his hands. But all was gloriously quiet.

Delving without a skill was common at lower levels, but the casualty rate was much higher for those unlucky delvers.

Matt already decided he wouldn't let this pad out of his sight for the remainder of the year. This skill was near perfect for him. A channeled skill would allow him to use his full 1 mana per second of mana generation while he was under 0.1 mana.

Matt used his PlanetNet voucher time to check on the status of the Glesie public rift. The purchase price for a spot was still ten thousand credits and holding steady.

A while back, it had spiked to eleven thousand for a few weeks before dropping to nine thousand for a bit. Now, it was back at its usual price. He then quickly searched for average mana stats for lower Tier mages and found a guide put out by the Juniper family that had the barony over the planet.

The guide was only recommended up to Tier 3, then more advanced versions had to be purchased. It focused on directed mana cultivation and its three aspects: Maximum Mana, Mana Regeneration, and Mana Concentration.

Fascinated, Matt read on. The orphanage hadn't covered the nuances of directed cultivation. They taught that as you gathered essence from killing monsters in rifts, the person dealing the final hit absorbed the lion's share of the essence.

Most teams wore devices that automatically divided the essence amongst the rest of the party. Ratios could even be changed so one person could get nearly all the essence, which was how crafters got the necessary essence to advance without having the skills to fight monsters themselves.

Once out of the rift, you would process the essence, allocating it to either your body or mana.

Cultivators could direct how they allocated the essence. Physical and mana were the two sides of cultivation. After that choice, you could target sub aspects of each, which was called 'directed cultivation,'

The other option was to let the essence go where it was needed, called undirected cultivation. It was an easy way to shore up weak areas.

The guide described directed cultivation as making mountains to have specialization and letting the valleys get filled in, raising the baseline to build your peaks even higher, is called undirected cultivation.

All power needed a strong foundation, after all.

None of these details were discussed at the orphanage. They were just told that the group they joined would have their own guidelines and recommendations specific to their position.

The guide said the goal at Tier 3 was to have 1,000 mana and Mana Regeneration of about one mana every two and a half minutes. The guide explained this was the ideal ratio for directed mana cultivation at lower levels, with 70% directed mana cultivation and 30% undirected physical.

The guide strongly warned against attempting directed physical cultivation until Tier 3, and only when the appropriate classes were taken. The guides specifically for it were not available until after the classes were taken.

What's the difference? Why are you allowed directed mana cultivation but not physical at Tier 1? Matt wondered but got back to reading. The information was interesting but not particularly useful until he could collect essence in a rift. It was still something to do, so he kept reading while he couldn't sleep.

The general idea was that a mage would regenerate 576 mana a day. It also wasn't recommended to delve more than once every three days, and delve slots reflected that. That would let mages fully regenerate their mana pool in under two days. That extra mana could then be used for practicing their skills or stored in rechargeable mana stones for quick mana recharges in a rift.

The rechargeable mana stones were particularly recommended. Because it was mana from your own mana pool, there wouldn't be any time needed to aspect

the mana to match your natural mana pool. The guide also recommended emptying and refilling any low Tier rechargeable mana stones after a week because the mana would un-aspect, turning into ambient mana.

Un-aspected mana was great for powering devices but was hell on a cultivator's mana channels. Directly using it could cause near permanent damage.

The last and most interesting part of the guide covered Mana Concentration. Allocating any essence into Mana Concentration before Tier 5 was flatly not recommended.

Mana Concentration shrunk your other mana cultivation aspects to make your mana denser and more concentrated. Denser mana gave your spells more power for the same cost, but the returns were terrible.

To double the power of a spell with Mana Concentration, a Tier 5 mage would need to diminish their base Maximum Mana and Mana Regeneration values back to what they had at Tier 1. That was at a 70% essence allocation to mana through all the preceding Tiers.

That brought Matt up short.

What an insanely bad return.

The amount of essence a Tier 5 had would be massive. In the early Tiers, advancing to the next Tier required ten times the essence of the previous one. If it took ten essence to reach the peak of Tier 1, then it took a hundred to reach the peak of Tier 2.

It was why people didn't farm low Tier rifts despite them being safer. The monsters didn't have enough essence to make it worthwhile. Killing a single monster in a Tier 2 rift was worth the equivalent of killing a dozen in a Tier 1 rift.

The amount of mana and Mana Regeneration a Tier 5 mage would have would be insane, completely incomparable to a Tier 3. Doubling the power of each skill would force them to give all of that up to reset back to the base of around 100 mana and one mana every twenty minutes.

Mana Concentration, for all its downsides, was an important part of mana cultivation. Maximum Mana and Mana Regeneration had diminishing returns when applied to the allocated essence after a certain point. The spirit could only grow so much without strain, and Mana Concentration increased that cap farther than the cultivators lost from Maximum Mana and Mana Regeneration when allocating to it, eventually allowing a mage to have millions of mana.

Which just proved going from Tier 5 mana levels to Tier 1 wasn't worth it. But, then again, this guide was tailored for lower Tier mages. Matt doubted this was the whole truth.

It was a good warning, though. Matt was sure many a young mage would have crippled their mana cultivation early on without that warning. They would be in the same boat as Matt, unable to cast a single spell but without his advantages.

Matt stroked his pad. His Tier 1 Talent wasn't perfect, but this skill shard synergized with it amazingly.

Before falling asleep, he plugged the pad in so the mana battery would charge overnight and tried to drift off.

The vibration of his pad woke Matt up. It was 3:55 a.m. Panicked, Matt clumsily tapped around the pad, finally opening a video to hear nothing. Sighing, he flopped back to his bed.

All was well. The skill shard hadn't managed to run off in the night somehow. It hadn't all been a dream. Still exhausted, he forced himself to get moving. Midnight had been rolling around when he'd finally fallen asleep.

I can nap during the day in the maintenance room.

Despite his weariness, he arrived at the training room only a smidgeon late. According to his schedule, today was only flexibility training. If it had been a strength training day, Matt didn't know how he would have done anything. Stretching was a perfect way to wake himself up before Dena and Eric came down to spar.

When they arrived, both headed straight to his corner. Matt was surprised. Eric had recently said his control training was almost done, so he was doubling down on the practice to get it over with quicker.

As soon as they got close, Eric announced, "Matt, Dena and I talked it over last night. You have talent, and it's wasted here. We want to help."

Matt started to say it wasn't necessary. He didn't want to take charity from them. They were too kind. It would make him feel dirty.

He thought back to last night, the skill shard he'd swiped. Did he still even deserve help after that? If it had been theirs, he knew he wouldn't have stolen it. The arrogant stranger was another matter.

Before he could get anything out, Eric continued, "It's not charity. You're going to earn it in a spar. Unless they have a Talent that boosts physical cultivation, a Tier 1 fighter just landing a hit on a Tier 3 is more than enough to earn them a guild invitation. Anywhere but here, at least. It's actually a pretty standard test in the Empire proper. Though they usually make the fight against a peak Tier 2 with a 70% split."

Dena returned from the weapons rack with a pair of blunted daggers.

Instinctively, Matt wanted to reject her offer. On the other hand, though, this might be his best shot at escape from this shit hole city. He wouldn't need to spend another nine months slaving away. He could escape with his stolen skill shard all the sooner.

Dena clearly saw his internal struggle because she preempted, "Remember, this isn't charity. You're either going to earn the hit or not. And I'll be fighting at Tier 3 strength and speed."

The hesitation didn't completely disappear from Matt's face, so Eric followed up, "We won't force you, but sponsoring a young talent isn't unheard of. It's really not that uncommon in the Empire proper. You're hardly the first person to ever come out of the Awakening with a... *less than ideal* Tier 1 Talent. The Emperor doesn't want potentially strong people to languish in the gutters because they were born on low Tier planets or with weak Talents."

"That's where the Path of Ascension comes in. A sponsor even gets rewarded if their sponsee does well. Make it to Tier 5, we get some small rewards. Make it to Tier 10, we keep getting more and more, all the way up to Tier 25."

Eric looked wistful as he continued, "The Empire *wants* powerhouses, *needs* them. But it also won't waste resources on those who won't put them to good use.

This system helps all involved, but we won't recommend anyone if they don't have the drive to advance."

Matt swallowed. It didn't sound like he'd be taking advantage of them. But what would happen if he didn't do well?

Dena anticipated his question. "If you stop advancing or die before Tier 5, you simply get marked as a failure. If a sponsor has too many failed recommendations on their record, they lose the ability to sponsor more people. That's really just in place to stop people from recommending everyone they see to play the odds."

A final bit of reticence held Matt back, so Eric added, "This moment right here, this is exactly how we got started, two street rats from a Tier 5 planet. Someone saw potential and gave us a chance to prove ourselves. There are thousands of low Tier planets in the Empire, Matt. More great people than you probably think come from places like this."

He and Dena shared a smile, reminiscing on their own beginnings.

That decided it for Matt. "All right. I'll do it. I'll rise all the way to Tier 25 eventually and get you those rewards." Matt tightened his grip on the training longsword. Who didn't want to complete The Path? Who didn't want to be a legend?

Dena laughed. "That's the spirit!"

With that, she lunged at him and started the most intense fight of Matt's life. She moved faster than in any previous spar. Matt strained his eyes just trying to make out some of her movements. They were mere flickers that left lines of pain in their wake.

As the five-minute mark passed, Matt realized there wouldn't be rounds between engagements to catch his

breath in or rethink his strategy. This would only end when he gave up or landed a hit.

Matt's resolve hardened. He hadn't chanced stealing the skill shard because he was afraid of a risk or a challenge. He could take some risks in a spar. So, he concentrated on keeping his movement defensive, disregarding Dena's strength and speed advantage. Her Tier 5 endurance meant she could just attack at full speed until he collapsed. Even if she kept her speed to a Tier 3.

Matt sent out more attacks, probing his opponent. His was the longer blade, so offense was his best defense. When she closed in, her more maneuverable daggers had the advantage. One could tie down his blade while she got in vicious stabs with the other.

Switching his attacking pattern bought Matt some breathing room. With a moment to think, he concluded Dena's lack of skill with her staff did not extend to her daggers. The woman had mentioned she preferred them as her main weapon, and it showed. She was intimately familiar with her range and light on her feet, which let her evade every blow as if she saw the future.

Matt stayed patient. He wasn't trying to kill her just land a single blow. Not an easy feat on someone with much higher physical abilities than a Tier 1 like him. While each Tier didn't quite double the power, if two people had the same allocation ratios, the difference was significant.

Higher Tier meant more essence. More essence meant more power.

The golden rule stated total essence distributed equaled increased power. It was the reason the higher Tiers required more than ten times the essence to rank

up and was also why the higher Tiers had such massive jumps in power between them.

After another few exchanges, the fight stalled. Dena was content with sending probing attacks or blocking with her daggers or forearm guards.

The more the fight dragged on, the more the fatigue and desperation set in. His energy was flagging. Running himself dry would spell the end of this chance. There was only one choice left; he had to go for broke, attacking with everything he had left at once.

Disregarding defense and leaning to a fully offensive strategy, he no longer conserved his energy and, instead, bet everything on the exchange. He tried to push her into a particular trap without being too obvious. The flurry of blows kept Dena on the defensive until Matt used the rebound of her blocking a side slash to step left and forward, closing in on her. He brought the longsword around with every last drop of power and speed he could muster.

Matt was 5'10, and Dena was only 5'8, maybe 5'9. It meant Matt held the slightest reach advantage even before their weapon choice came into play. Dena was more experienced and faster than him, though. As the blade swept in, she danced back from the blow.

His desperate plan failed. Matt wanted to curse but couldn't waste the breath. As he surged forward to follow up, Dena just kept retreating, holding her hands up.

Matt halted, fear gripping him.

I didn't hit her. Is she just calling it now because I wasn't good enough?

The next words he heard shocked him, "Well done, Matt! I knew you had it in you."

Off to the side, Eric even clapped a few times.

Matt was flabbergasted. He missed. They claimed it wasn't charity, but what was this obvious faking of a hit? At least they could have made it more convincing.

"I didn't hit you, though?" Matt protested. Somehow, charity from these two felt worse than failure.

Dena grinned broadly and raised her right arm to reveal her side. "Think again! You grazed me right here."

Matt saw nothing, but Eric nodded right along.

"You don't have to sponsor me. I couldn't make my part of the deal, so you don't have to feel—"

"Matt! You *did* hit me. Look!"

Dena reached down and pulled the workout shirt over her head. Matt couldn't help but stare, she was only wearing a sports bra now, and she had a light sheen of perspiration on her athletic body that reflected the light. She had freckles that ran down her upper chest down to her—

Matt jerked his eyes up to meet their combined smirks and felt his face flush hot.

Pale skin and a trail of freckles tempted him to look down again but, with an effort of willpower he didn't know he had, Matt kept his eyes on hers.

Dena had righted the shirt and showed him a small mark under the right armpit. Matt had to squint, but he could see it, if barely. A small diagonal line was only distinguishable from the fabric's weave because it didn't run parallel.

He *had* done it!

That was truly the smallest of strikes, but it was all he needed. Relief washed through him. As the stress of failing left him, his body wanted to collapse, being hopped up on adrenaline no longer enough to keep him standing.

Matt turned to Eric and Dena's smiling faces. Eric tossed Matt a small bag he definitely hadn't been holding before. "Well, congratulations, Matt. You did what most can't even dream of. Striking a person two Tiers up is one hell of an accomplishment."

"I don't know how I can repay you both."

Dena waved him off before he could continue. "Advancing will be more than enough thanks. Let alone the rewards we'll get the more you progress. But if you really want to pay us back, pay it forward once you get the chance. When you get to Tier 5, you can recommend someone for the same program. Don't waste it, but don't forget about it either."

"In the bag, I left you more instructions and a train ticket."

As Eric spoke, Matt managed to turn to him. Keeping his eyes off the woman standing not two feet away was a challenge.

Eric didn't seem to mind. "Though, you might want to get moving. The train leaves at eight, and the station isn't exactly next door. Unless you'd like to spend more time here, maybe?"

That statement cut through the cacophony of thoughts in Matt's head.

Not next door... That's an understatement. If I leave now, I'll still have to run at least part way to make it.

Matt gaped at them, unable to express his gratitude.

Dena took pity on him. "Best get a move on. I know I look *good*, but I don't think I look so good you'd pass up an opportunity to bail on this dump."

Matt flushed hot again, but her teasing also spurred him into action. Calling his thanks over his shoulder, Matt snatched up the pad from next to the wall and ran to his room. Then he had to find Benny to tell him he was done.

Freedom awaited.

Matt dashed down the road. A train couldn't be seen in the station, and he was terrified it had arrived and left early. Checking the pad clenched in his hands, the time only said 7:32 a.m., but he couldn't shake the fear he'd be stranded here.

He pulled up to the station with a torrent of sweat rolling down his back. Bouncing on his back was the pack holding his clothes and the few other possessions he had to his name.

He joined the small line at the teller's booth. As he waited, Matt opened the small bag Eric had tossed to him. Inside was an envelope and a few other odds and ends. At the bottom, hidden by the envelope, he found the train ticket.

After retrieving the precious paper, Matt carefully closed the pouch and waited his turn. He'd explore the other contents of the bag later when he could sit and dedicate his full attention to it.

When the person in front of him walked to the waiting area, Matt moved forward and handed the ticket over to the man behind the glass. The clerk scanned it and reviewed their screen. "One cabin to Durham. No transfers. Do you have any luggage you want to check

into storage?" The man's eyes never even peeked away from his screen while he recited the question.

"No, thank you."

"Well, in that case, you have a four-day trip ahead of you. Two meals will be provided per day. You can choose what meals you take. You'll have to go to the food cars near the front and rear of the train. Any questions?" The man mechanically pushed a new slip of paper out of the small window, his attention still not wandering from the screen.

Matt took the slip, said he didn't, and thanked the man before walking to the seating area.

With no train in sight, he stowed the boarding pass in the pocket with his pad and found a restroom to freshen up. His earlier sparring session and run to the station had left him in a grimy state.

Keeping an ear out for his train's announcement, Matt hurried through his ablutions, still anxious he'd miss the train. After only another ten minutes of tense waiting, the train finally pulled into the station. Only a few people departed, and then the boarding call started.

Handing his pass to the man at the door, he was directed to car twelve, room two. Matching the room number to the one on his boarding pass, Matt was prompted to scan his pass and pair the door key with his pad or AI to secure the room from unwanted guests.

The room was small but more than enough for his uses. Matt dropped his pack of clothes to the side and carefully poured the contents of Eric's pouch onto the bed.

Starting with the envelope, Matt opened it and read the letter inside.

Matt,

We are so happy you earned this opportunity. You are hard-working and dedicated to improving yourself, traits rarer than you probably think. We will be leaving as soon as you are on your way, so don't bother trying to find us. It's harsh, but if you have too much contact with your sponsor, it spoils a lot of sponsees. You are meant to find your own path. It's called The Path of Ascension because it's only wide enough for one. Don't be afraid to make unconventional choices. Learn from others but don't treat anyone's advice like it's the only truth, even this advice.

You are on a good start, believe it or not. You may think you're behind because you spent a year working at Benny's, but most places don't perform the Awakening ceremony until late fourteen at the earliest, anyway, and don't let people delve until fifteen. Emotional maturity will keep you alive in a rift as much as strength once you arrive at the PlayPen.

Matt was struck dumb. Arrive at the PlayPen? It was true, then. A part of him had thought they'd be covering the ten thousand credits to get a delve slot, not getting him into the PlayPen, no matter what they had said. He still remembered how Miles talked about the PlayPen like a desire that couldn't be fulfilled.

He continued reading.

> *Once you arrive at the PlayPen, take the intro course and what they recommend there. It's been quite a while since we were under Tier 3, so it's a little fuzzy, but only the best are chosen to staff a PlayPen. It's a prestigious position, even on a low Tier world like Lilly. You can trust their advice, though you should think critically about everything you hear.*
>
> *I do recall you will get a slot in the rift once every three days. Be careful. They will have true healers on staff, but it's expensive. Though you shouldn't have a problem with getting injured with your skills if you are careful and patient. We gave you permission to immediately start delving because, with your combat ability, it shouldn't be hard for you to solo a Tier 1 rift. If you don't get cocky.*
>
> *Well, and that skill shard you swiped should help a lot.*

The letter slipped from his hands. The earlier shock at going to the PlayPen was replaced with dread.

They saw that and still gave me this?

Matt gulped and, with far more nerves than before, continued.

> *Well, and that skill shard you swiped should help a lot. It's a good skill to pair with your Talent and, no, sponsors can't see a sponsee's Tier 1 Talent until they are*

accepted, but we can feel your mana pool when you use items. Eric and I both feel that, even if you don't get a paired Tier 3 Talent, you can strive to get the Tier 25 Talent, even with this handicap. Though we find it unlikely. AND DON'T DIRECT CULTIVATE PHYSICAL UNTIL TIER 3!!!!!

Back to the shard, don't feel bad. You took an opportunity placed in front of you and made it out successfully. Being willing to take a risk is important, and knowing your limits is crucial. You took both into account and won. Besides, if the idiot didn't make a scene and throw a fucking expensive skill shard to start a brawl, he wouldn't have lost it.

That's on him, and if you hadn't tried to get the old man out of harm's way at the cost of your own safety, you wouldn't have been in the position to profit. Karma was working fast yesterday.

The handwriting style changed and became sloppier.

Eric here. That was a slick palming. The only reason I noticed (Dena completely missed it!!!) was because we were watching to make sure no one killed you by accident. But it was a good plan, and well-executed!! Just had to say that. Good luck and visit the—

Whatever the last word Eric had tried to write had been scratched out to the point it was illegible. And the handwriting went back to the loopy style of Dena.

> Don't go to places like that. He's just trying to live vicariously through you because he knows if he went to one, I'd go to one in revenge, and neither one of us wants that.

Matt had to pause.
What the hell are they talking about?

> Anyway, good luck. You got this.
> Best Wishes,
> Dena and Eric Thorne.
> PS: I forgot because of Eric stealing the pen. Look up 'the curve.' It will be informative. While you're on the train, just focus on absorbing the skill shard. When you get to the PlayPen, buy a newer pad. The ones they sell there are Empire standard, and that means they're twenty-plus years ahead of the best this planet otherwise has.
> PPS: Also, the card has a 20k limit, so buy a good weapon and don't be afraid to go

> into a bit of debt in the beginning. The PlayPen should have a budgeting class. Take it.
> PPPS: PSs are fun.

Matt was surprised to hear they'd been watching out for him in the brawl. He hadn't been looking for them but, then again, he hadn't seen them either. It felt good, like a warmth in his chest he hadn't known since before the rift break.

Playing with the piece of plastic, he inspected the credit card. He'd never even thought of owning one before. No bank would risk loaning to someone under Tier 3 or without a backer.

Which I guess I have now.

Now, he had a credit limit twice what it would have cost to buy a slot in Glesie. It felt unreal.

Matt inspected the last few things in the bag. One was the mana control ball Eric had been practicing with for so long. It was a nice gesture, and a good reminder that even if he couldn't allocate into his mana cultivation, he could still work on control.

Once he got more mana, that was.

For the first time, that didn't sound like an outlandish dream. Two Tier 5s thought the problem would fix itself with his Tier 3 Talent, and he trusted their expertise more than his own.

The last gift was a pair of gloves like the ones he saw Dena use but in his size.

Are they special?

Matt tried them on and couldn't see anything different about them. Knowing those two, though, he trusted they were useful. Even if just as normal gloves, he'd cherish everything they gave him. Because of them, he had a chance at true freedom. Even before the sponsorship and as strangers, they'd treated him better than most people in his life.

Matt repacked the items and went to retrieve his skill shard from his pad but came to the realization he didn't have anything flat and hard enough to pry the back off. After scouring the room and finding nothing, he briefly debated smashing the pad to get the back off to get his skill shard out.

Opting instead to be reasonable, he trekked over to the dining car and, finding it empty, grabbed a pre-packaged meal and utensils. After eating, he dumped his tray into the disposable rack while pocketing the unused knife.

Back in his cabin, the pilfered knife was used to get the pad open and retrieve the skill shard.

With it in hand, Matt reassembled the pad before realizing he didn't know exactly how to absorb the skill. No one ever discussed the details. People acted like it was self-explanatory, but Matt was clueless about where to begin. Fear seeped in that he would somehow ruin the skill by experimenting.

Matt opened the PlanetNet and quickly found a guide. It wasn't free, but only cost one hundred credits. He had six thousand credits saved from Benny's and a credit limit of twenty thousand. Still, he paused.

Why am I worried about such a small price?

With warring instincts, Matt inputted his account information and waited as the purchase was verified.

As Matt read the guide, he was glad he purchased it. The actual process of absorbing a skill was easy, just send

a strand of essence to the skill, and it would flow into your spirit.

According to the guide, there were three ways to absorb a skill. Or rather, three different functional degrees of distance you could pull the skill into your spirit, which was the determining factor on how long a skill took to absorb.

The first example was called core skills according to the guide. The number of such skills your spirit could hold depended on Tier but could also be influenced by Talents. However, on average, Tier 1 people could hold two skills in the core spirit.

The limited number was made up for by a notable boost. Skills in the core generally saw around a 30% boost to some combination of their efficiency, power, and casting speed. Being in the core of the spirit also allowed the skill to be modified by the user far more easily. It was recommended that build defining skills or lifesaving skills went to the core spirit.

There was a trade-off, though. Even at Tier 5, most people only had three slots, and then at Tier 10, four. Every tenth Tier after that allowed for one more as the spirit grew with cultivation.

Next was the inner spirit. This was where the average skill was presumed to be added to. At Tier 1, six slots were the norm, with two more being added with each new Tier. The inner spirit was the place general combat skills were recommended. Space was plentiful enough that most wouldn't have enough skills to even fill it as they advanced. It was the average, the baseline everything else was judged on.

The outer spirit was last. By far the largest area, it had room for twenty skills at Tier 1 and expanded enough for five more each Tier. The skills located here were slower and weaker by about half, with the mana cost also going up 50% on average. Non-combat spells like [Purify], [Cleanse], or [Create Water] were often put there. Skills that, while useful, were not time-critical to cast.

According to the guide, while skills could be shifted around the spirit after initial absorption, it took months of deliberate meditation.

Finally, and most importantly, was how long it took to get the skill into each of the spirit's areas. About a day was required per area it moved through, starting with the outer spirit. That rate would be slightly sped up by Tier. So long as the shard constantly had essence circulating, the skill was considered to be in the integration phase and would slowly move closer to the core region.

The guide explained he should feel the difference as the skill moved along, and its progress through his spirit would give him a good example of the core, inner, and outer regions of the spirit.

Learning all this, Matt was relieved he bought the guide. He'd never heard anything about this and was sure he'd have ended up with his single very synergistic skill languishing in the outer spirit without the guide, losing out on a ton of power.

The guide recommended skills being absorbed should be secured to the body with specially made holders so they couldn't be stolen or dropped.

Matt taped it to his chest.

Once the shard was secured, he directed a strand of essence to the shard and felt the process take over. The skill shard seemed to gently pull his essence while feeding back the essence after circulating through the shard, completely automated. He just had to be mindful of his chest until the skill moved to the core of his spirit.

The next day, Matt felt a jolt in his spirit. He instantly knew that if he directed mana through the skill structure still moving in his spirit, he'd activate the skill [Cracked Phantom Armor]. With a day-long grin, he anticipated the arrival at Durham and then the PlayPen in two more days.

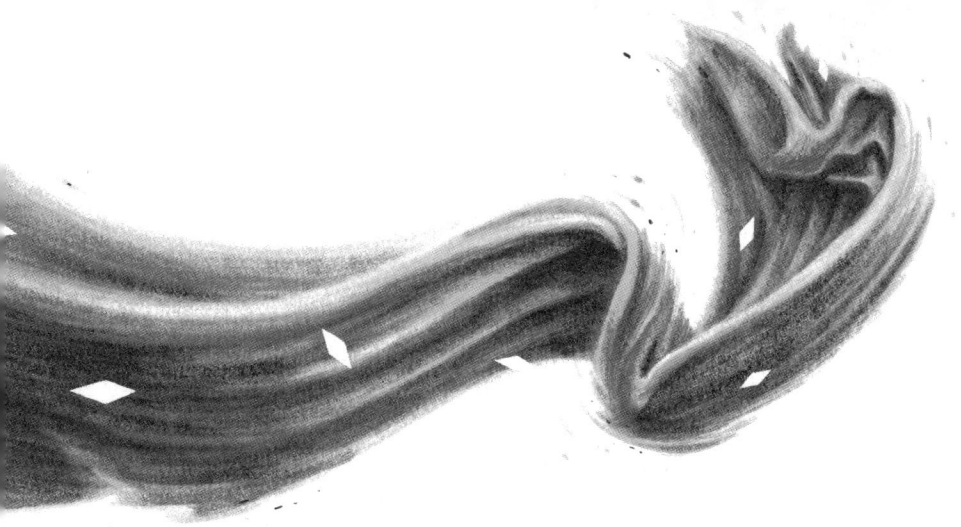

Chapter 4

Durham and the PlayPen were still a day out when Matt felt the final jolt in his spirit that signaled [Cracked Phantom Armor] reached his core spirit.

The skill's structure stuck out to him in his spirit. Like an infinitely complex 3D blueprint, it sat waiting to be used, begging Matt to try out the skill.

His first skill.

Knowing he couldn't test the skill was eating him alive. Using a skill outside of designated areas was automatically considered a hostile action. No one wanted a stray [Fireball] to burn down a building or injure someone, so cities enforced a blanket ban on the activation of all combat related skills. Sadly, that included even defensive skills. Matt had checked, twice.

Resigned to having to wait until he reached the PlayPen and their training grounds to see what his skill could do, Matt tried to relax. But after the last year and a half at Benny's, he could scarcely remember what free

time was. Without another outlet for his attention, he just pondered his new skill.

The skill would be better than most, Matt was confident. One mana a second into a channeling skill was far more than a normal mage could reasonably maintain. They would eat heavily into their mana reserves pulling something like that off, even for a short time.

The situation just grated. Everything he dreamed of was within his grasp, but he was still stuck waiting.

Trying to spend his time productively, Matt searched the PlanetNet for anything he could learn about the PlayPen. There wasn't much information readily available.

The only guide cost two thousand credits, and when reading the reviews, he found one stating the author deleted any negative ones. Considering Matt couldn't find any negative reviews, he deemed it fishy enough that he wouldn't risk that many credits.

What public information Matt found was sparse and only general to all PlayPens, not the particular one in Durham. PlayPens were manmade islands that used the five-mile safe zone between the essence convergence of land and water to create an island that had Tier 1, 2, and 3 rifts.

They would then dump mana to force rifts to form. If the rift had an acceptable monster type and didn't have any peculiarities, they kept it. Otherwise, teams would delve the rift until it lost enough essence and mana it dissipated, or they drained the area, but that was said to be much harder.

A PlayPen was incredibly expensive to build, and then just as costly to maintain on a low Tiered world. The rifts had to be supplied with mana stones because the ambient

mana and essence that fueled the rifts wasn't enough to keep up with the rate of delving PlayPens needed. Some speculation Matt saw said it cost more than a Tier 6 mana stone per day to run a PlayPen.

That explained why others didn't copy the method. A Tier 1 mana stone alone was worth one hundred credits. From there, each higher Tier increased in value by tenfold until Tier 5, when the value jumped by fifty-fold each time. That put the speculated cost of maintaining the PlayPen's rifts at a quarter billion credits *per day*.

An unfathomable number to Matt, who'd made just four hundred credits a month.

That number completely disregarded the cost of the facilities the Empire staffed, said to be state of the art, with top-of-the-line technology. In total, it might cost double that to run.

The sheer amount of money was unbelievable. It made Matt even more grateful Dena and Eric got him in.

When Durham came into view, Matt was ready and waiting at one of the doors of the train, bag over his shoulder. Stepping off the train, a rush of people trying to board confronted him, fighting against the tide of people trying to leave.

Once through the crush of bodies, he saw a tall man holding up two signs. One read 'Darius Blackwell,' and the other had his name, 'Matthew Alexander,'

Matt walked over to the man. As he approached, the stranger glanced at him, and then down to a pad. After looking back and forth, he said, "You're here. Good. Try to find the other guy." He turned his pad around and revealed two pictures, one of Matt and another of a stern-faced youth with black hair and silver eyes.

The other young man had almost the exact opposite features of Matt. Where the man was dark, Matt was light. His own hair was sandy blond, and he had green eyes that trended to hazel at the edges.

A minute later, they found Darius had waited for the rush to end, and he walked out as the doors were closing. Bag rolling behind him, he quickly spotted his name on the sign being held up.

"Okay, good. You two are the only new entries to the PlayPen this week. The name's Griff, and I'm the second in command here. Tier 15. I've been an active delver for the last ninety years. A bit slower than The Path but better slow than dead." He paused for a moment. "I'm here as a break and to raise my kid. He just turned one. You gotta see him. He just took his first steps. I have to show you. It was so cute."

Griff then showed the two newcomers far more pictures of a small child than Matt felt necessary. He wished the man would get back to talking about the PlayPen. Any nerves about being near the strongest person Matt ever met quickly vanished as Griff swiped through pictures of his kid on his pad and accompanied each with a story of his kid's antics.

After various compliments from the boys, Griff returned to the subject of the PlayPen. "Sorry about that. Me and the wife have been waiting forever to hit Tier 15 and have a kid. Having a kid before Tier 15 is a great

way to kill your momentum as a delver. After Tier 15, you have all the time in the world. Immortality, it's a beautiful feeling not having to worry about old age."

Matt was envious. Immortality and Tier 15 seemed so far away, it hurt. And Griff had done it in around one hundred years. That answered why he only looked to be in his mid-twenties. Matt wasn't sure how that was 'a *little slow.*' It seemed fast to him. Matt craved that, and a glance at Darius showed the same look on his face.

"So, we have a few things to do before we board the boat to the island. It shouldn't take long."

The few things Griff needed to do was shop for baby things. Massive amounts of clothes and toys were purchased. Matt assumed the Tier 15 was loaded because, if his running calculations were close, Griff spent one hundred thousand credits in the two hours.

It made Matt look up the mana stone to credit chart up to Tier 15.

Tier of Mana Stone	Credits per Mana Stone	Mana Stones to Next Tier
Tier 1	100	10
Tier 2	1,000	10
Tier 3	10,000	10
Tier 4	100,000	10
Tier 5	5,000,000	50
Tier 6	250,000,000	50
Tier 7	12,500,000,000	50
Tier 8	625,000,000,000	50
Tier 9	31,250,000,000,000	50

Tier 10	3,125,000,000,000,000	100
Tier 11	312,500,000,000,000,000	100
Tier 12	31,250,000,000,000,000,000	100
Tier 13	3,125,000,000,000,000,000,000	100
Tier 14	312,500,000,000,000,000,000,000	100
Tier 15	31,250,000,000,000,000,000,000,000	100

It boggled his mind that a single mana stone could be worth so much. The little information he found on the CityNet said after Tier 5 most people didn't use credits as a currency but the mana stones themselves.

He could only assume all spending was like throwing away spare change to the Tier 15.

All the purchases were absorbed into the ring on his finger. When Darius asked, Griff said, "It's a spatial ring. Can't use one till your Tier 15 because of the strain it puts on your spirit. But, damn, are they useful. Don't worry too much, you'll get there one day."

Matt felt that by the end of the shopping trip, he and Darius were far closer from the constantly shared looks of envy and awe at Griff's spending.

Finally, after what felt like hours, they boarded a small, sleek boat.

Once the boat was underway, Griff talked more about the PlayPen. "So, you're both sponsored and on The Path, which has some benefits and limitations."

At their questioning looks, Griff continued, "You get better discounts and top priority at all facilities on the island and preferential treatment in most larger establishments throughout the Empire. The limitations are all about 'The Curve' and teaming up with others

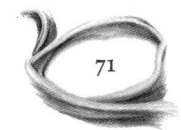

outside of The Path." Matt could hear the capital letters in the words.

Darius asked the question Matt was thinking, "My sponsor mentioned that, but I wasn't able to find anything on the PlanetNet about it." Neither had Matt, so he wanted this answered as well.

"Yeah, you'll need access to the EmpireNet to have access to information like that. Only sponsees are on The Path here, so no need to make everyone else feel inferior. The curve is how The Path of Ascension is graded. It's an Empire-wide race to the top. 80% of people will fall behind after Tier 5, and the rest are true powerhouses. Future pillars of the Empire."

Griff looked around. "It's hard. You have to keep ascending Tiers fast, really fast. Tier 3 by seventeen is easy, but Tier 5 by twenty-one is a bit harder, Tier 10 by thirty-nine is absurd for most people."

Matt swallowed. That *was* absurd, by what he knew of this planet, at least.

"It's easier to show you." With that, Griff tapped at his pad, sending Matt a message.

The Path	Reached By
Tier 1	15
Tier 2	16
Tier 3	17
Tier 4	19
Tier 5	21
Tier 6	24
Tier 7	27

Tier	
Tier 8	31
Tier 9	35
Tier 10	39
Tier 11	44
Tier 12	49
Tier 13	55
Tier 14	62
Tier 15	69
Tier 16	78
Tier 17	88
Tier 18	98
Tier 19	110
Tier 20	123
Tier 21	138
Tier 22	153
Tier 23	168
Tier 24	183
Tier 25	200

Matt had no frame of reference for the numbers. It seemed impossible to reach Tier 25 before turning two hundred. He hadn't even heard of people reaching Tier 3 before their mid-twenties.

"And, no, you can't just have a guild or noble family power level you or give you resources. That's a part of the restrictions. While you can join a guild, you can't take anything from them. Can't even use guild-owned rifts without paying the public price yourself. It's meant to be a solo climb, and most just can't keep up, but those who do are stronger than anyone else at their Tier."

Griff looked out over the sea for a long moment before he cleared his throat and continued, "If you stay on The Path, the rewards are immense. There are tournaments for only those still competing, and the prizes are beyond your imagination. Speaking of prizes, if you are still on The Path, your sponsor's rewards are equally absurd.

"The finish line is Tier 25 by age two hundred. By the end, you have to ascend a Tier every fifteen years." Griff shook his head. "My whole party fell off at Tier 10.

"It's easier for solo delvers in the lower Tiers as you don't have to split the essence, which helps a lot. Even then, my party was delving every two days. Everyone who makes it past Tier 10 is delving rifts at least one Tier higher than themselves. It's dangerous and gets many a—" Griff made finger quotes, "'genius' killed because it's hard.

"I won't tell you not to push to stay ahead of the curve. I even encourage it! At least until Tier 5. But, after that, take a good hard look at yourself and ask if it's worth it."

Griff mentioned rewards better than he could imagine. His imagination was pretty big, so he had to ask, "What's the reward for getting to Tier 25 while on The Path?"

Griff sighed as he answered, "The last person to hit Tier 25 was Duke Waters. He wasn't a duke at that point, but he was given the title and a Tier 35 world as a personal fiefdom and management over nearly sixty other worlds. All under his command. His sponsors were rumored to have gotten a Tier 30 world as well, but that's not confirmed as they never went public. He was also given access to the Emperor's own vault and was kitted out with the best skills and equipment."

Matt took it back. His imagination wasn't nearly big enough. He had seen movies about Duke Waters. The man was a living legend.

Darius asked a question Matt hadn't considered, "Isn't a Tier 25 far too weak to rule a Tier 35 world? Wouldn't those under his rule be discontent being ruled by someone so much weaker than them?"

That made Griff laugh. "Yeah, a few thought the same thing and sent their sons to try and duel him. They thought they could get him out of the way by sending from Tier 27s up to low Tier 30s to *accidentally* kill him. Those who went are called the lost generation now. He killed every single one who stepped up. When their parents sought revenge, the Emperor himself stepped in and told them to fuck off.

"Remember, he's the first person to ride The Path to the end in the last few thousand years or so. Duke Waters was soloing Tier 28 rifts to make it to Tier 25 before age two hundred. That's not remotely easy. Any man or woman crazy enough to do it *and* survive isn't someone to mess with."

The older man slapped his thigh. "All right, enough of that. We're almost at the PlayPen. When you get there, I'll take you to the administration building to get you both your Empire IDs and then medical. Gotta get your shots and birth control set up.

"After that, you both will be assigned delve slots. Since you're newcomers and it's the off-season, you shouldn't get night slots. We usually get waves of newcomers right after the school year ends, so it shouldn't be crowded for you right now. You've both been cleared by your sponsors to delve immediately, but I would talk to the Tier 2s and Tier 3s for advice before going into the rift. Killing your

first monster can be harder than most think. There are even simulations you can buy. I suggest it but can't force you. Just remember, there are no safety nets in the rifts."

The Tier 15 sighed out, "Any questions?"

Matt and Darius had none and, soon, they arrived at the island.

As Griff dropped them off at the administration building, he left them with one last piece of advice, "Don't delve more than once every three days. You can request and get more slots but don't. Take one day for the delve, one day for training, and one day for leisure and classes. That's the best schedule to go with at these Tiers to avoid burnout."

As he left, he gave them a hard look and finished, "Don't die, kids."

The admin process was easy enough. At one point, the clerk had them fill out identification cards. When giving the forms to Matt and Darius, he stressed that, if anything was wrong, it would be years of work to change, and this information took precedence over any other.

Matt noticed Darius inputting a different last name. He didn't feel it was necessary but assumed there was a story behind Darius's actions. Not that he would press the other teen on it.

Arriving off-cycle, Matt even got a delve slot for the next morning. After being assigned a room, he quickly went to a general store he'd seen on the way to the admin building. The place was massive and seemed to sell anything Matt could think of.

With only minimal searching, he found the pads and discovered they only sold a single model. Looking at the specs, it truly was better than anything on the open market. The pad was faster and more efficient than even the latest model on the local markets, let alone his current refurbished pad.

It not only had a battery that held twenty mana, which was ten times more than his current pad, but it could also slowly absorb ambient mana or be directly charged from the user. That took time for it to un-aspect the mana to ambient mana but was still amazing in longer delves.

The pad also came with permanent access to the EmpireNet so long as he was on The Path. The screen was even made from artificial mana stones, so it was scratch resistant to anything weaker than diamonds. It advertised so much storage he didn't think he could ever fill it.

All these features came with a corresponding cost, a whopping fifteen thousand credits.

As Matt was about to walk away, an employee approached him. "Are you a sponsee and on The Path? If you are, you get 50% off all indicated prices throughout the store, and the first pad you purchase is 80% off."

That information put Matt in a fantastic mood as he realized how much farther his money would go. He felt Griff had undersold the benefits of staying under the curve and on The Path.

With that good news, Matt's shopping spree began in earnest.

New pad, into the cart.

New boots, cart.

New well-fitting clothes both for delving and leisure, cart.

A new close fit backpack he could fit an emergency kit and water bladder in, cart.

Matt wandered the aisles and filled his cart with anything he thought would be useful.

As he was shopping, he found out what the gloves Dena had given him were. They were mage gloves. They let mana seamlessly pass through but blocked the physical manifestations from harming a mage; no burns from casting too many [Fireball]s. According to the packaging, they were a good unarmored alternative for melee fighters because of the same resistances.

He couldn't even find the same gloves she had given him, so he wasn't sure how much they cost. But he was, by examining the gloves, able to guess they were a higher quality than what they sold here.

The employee only suggested wearing them until Tier 3 because, after that, custom orders would be a better option. As at that point, enchantments would be available. It seemed like good advice, and Matt filed it away for later.

His final purchase was an essence accumulator. It was a thin bracelet that let parties share essence. It was what allowed mages and other backline fighters to collect essence without having to get in close and finish off monsters.

Matt was skeptical he needed it as a solo delver, but the clerk pointed out it improved essence accumulation, even if by only a few percent. It would still add up.

Pushing his overflowing cart to the checkout, Matt happily paid the five thousand credit cost and stopped by his room to drop off his goods. He then set up his new pad.

Once that was taken care of, Matt inputted his schedule. Before he could get too engrossed in playing with new features, he forced himself to change into his new combat clothes and head to the weapon shop.

When Matt entered, he noticed it wasn't a store like he expected but a workshop with at least a dozen active forges. There were twice that number as well, all sitting cold and empty.

A resting blacksmith near the entrance saw his obvious confusion and waved him down.

"You new here?"

At Matt's nod, he continued, "That means you're new on The Path. Makes it easy, then."

He waved at the surroundings. "The Path isn't only for combatants. There is a separate route for crafters. It's just as hard, but it's about what you can make not how fast you climb the Tiers. Though that's still a part of it. That's irrelevant, though. What you need to know is how this works. There are around forty blacksmiths on the island right now. No clue on the number of alchemists or other professions, but the same basics apply to all crafters in all professions."

He pointed at a screen in front of his area. "Any crafter has to have a sign with five pieces of information: their profession, their specialty, their Tier, the Tier of equipment they sell, and if they're on The Path currently.

"Blacksmiths usually display a shield with the weapon or type of armor they specialize in. That's two of the requirements right there. The border of the emblem will be gold if they're on The Path, silver if they were on The Path and fell off, and bronze if they never were on The Path. Then, they will usually spell out what Tiers they work with somewhere."

The sign was a gold shield with crossed daggers inside with a stylized '3' next to the arrangement. Underneath it was 'Smith's Ironworks and Enchantment.'

The smith is named Smith? What are the odds he changed his name?

Smith the *smith* smiled. "I've still got unenchanted works if you're in the market for a shortsword or daggers. Until you're Tier 3, I can't sell you any enchanted pieces." He gestured to a rack of beautifully made daggers.

"I will want a shield and some kind of single-handed weapon eventually, but I'm a longsword user first and foremost."

"Welp. I don't have those. If you want that, you should be fine in the rifts here with a longsword. No cramped spaces. Really, though, a dagger is always good to keep as a backup. I even have a leg sheath for you."

He pointed at a blade next to him on a shelf. "Here, for only three thousand."

Matt was tempted but didn't want to have to skimp on a longsword because he bought a backup weapon first. Matt only had fifteen thousand credits left on his card, and if the price of daggers indicated the price of a longsword, he would need all of it.

He was leery of dipping into what he had saved from Benny's. If he needed healing, he'd be screwed if he had neither credit available nor liquid funds.

When Matt said as much, Smith pointed him in the direction of the smiths who specialized in longswords. Thanking the man, he promised to come back for a dagger if he had the credits. He was proficient with the smaller blade, so it wouldn't be a wasted purchase, and a close range back up weapon wouldn't hurt to have.

Matt came to Tun's area next. The sign was a shield with gold trim, along with a longsword inside and an ornate three next to it.

When he approached the smithy, Tun was hammering away, so Matt browsed the displayed longswords. Finding the section with the length he preferred, he proceeded to test each one for weight and balance, carefully performing a few swings in the open area.

After a few minutes of debating between two similar swords, Matt was still undecided, and his preference was wavering between them. Both were good swords that fit him well enough. One was a tad shorter than he wanted but had superb balance. The other was slightly blade heavy and a little more expensive, but it was his preferred length.

As he pondered, the smith paused his work and approached with a hand held out. "Tun. I see you've got good taste. They're both good weapons, but that one was a commission where the other party never picked it up." The smith pointed at the blade heavy weapon.

Matt shook his hand and replied in kind, "Matt. And I was wondering why it's blade heavy. Clearly, it's not an accident."

Buttering up the person he was about to make a massive purchase from felt like a smart move, so he tried to flatter the man. He had enough practice with having to serve all the customers who worked at Benny's.

"Yeah, the guy wanted to have a heavier blade. Not a huge difference, but enough that it's been sitting there a while. Not many styles need a heavy blade that's not a bastard sword or greatsword.

"If you like it, I'll cut a thousand off the price. Even throw in a sheath for it."

The discount brought it down to the same price as the other weapon. Matt liked this blade slightly more than the shorter one, so that made the choice easier. He used blades balanced worse at Benny's, so it wouldn't be hard to change his style. The sheath was nice, but he would only use it while traveling as he wouldn't enter the rift without his weapon at the ready.

Still seeing Matt hesitating, Tun said, "Why don't you take it and test it out a bit. There's a small sparring room over here."

Small was an understatement. It was barely a broom closet, but it served its purpose. There was only one training aid that pivoted to focus on Matt as soon as he entered the room.

Exchanging a few blows, Matt decided he'd take the sword. It was a blade made for attack, and it sacrificed defensive speed to do so. But his singular skill was defensive, so the combination should mesh well. He still needed to test exactly how much damage the skill could block, and how [Cracked Phantom Armor] performed in simulated combat. But he was confident enough in his skills to take the risk of the heavy blade.

After completing his purchase for ten thousand credits, he stopped by Smith's and bought a cheaper dagger for a thousand. It was a simple curved dagger, so if his primary got stuck in a corpse, it would be easy to draw in a pinch.

Matt quickly scanned the provided map on his pad and found the training yard. It was a little after 4:30 p.m., and he wanted to get in a few hours of sparring and testing his [Cracked Phantom Armor] before tomorrow. Griff had suggested he wait, but the desire to finally progress after spinning his wheels at Benny's was too great.

As he arrived, he was almost run over by a group of six who came out the door right as Matt was opening it.

"Sorry, dude, bad timing on our part." The man in front was Matt's height and a year or so older, if he had to guess. "Hey, are you new? Don't recognize the face. Name's Mathew."

He ended his introduction by sticking out his hand.

"Mathew? Well, it's always nice to meet a fellow Matt." The Matts shook hands and each laughed.

"Well, now that I know you have good taste in names, we have to be best friends! So, new best friend, I'm assuming this is your first time at the training center?"

At Matt's nod, the older teen continued, "Well, let's give you the tour before we leave. By the Emperor's balls, we could have used a guide when we started." He then shook his hand back and forth. "Though we came on season, so it was slammed with Pathers and non-Pathers alike."

A tall blonde behind the older Mathew poked his side. "You're supposed to introduce the rest of your party, dumbass. I'm Melinda, that's Kyle, Sam, Vinnie, and Tara. Since Mathew is rude, I'll do the introductions. We are a sponsored team, high Tier 2."

After her introduction and handshake, Mathew looked sheepish and murmured, "I got excited at the name thing," before wilting further under Melinda's glare.

Melinda turned back to Matt. "You have new gear, and that's good, so you'll want to break it in." She pointed toward a hall lined with rooms. "That hall has the melee training rooms. So long as you're on The Path, they are free to use. And those..." she then pointed to another adjacent hall, "are the skill-testing halls. You can sync up your pad with the room to get training metrics and analysis of your fighting abilities and actual skills, if you

have any. It's useful, but if you want real improvement, go to that counter and hire a personal trainer."

Before Matt could say anything, she proceeded, "If you need a skill analysis, you need to talk to the front desk. They have testing rooms where you can get hard numbers on any skills you have."

Well, that's good to know.

"And that info is confidential, right?" Matt said before she could pass that comment by.

Mathew answered this time, "Yup. Only your sponsor can see that info, and only if you give them special permissions that they have to request."

"Thank you. You guys have been super helpful, I would have bumbled my way around until I figured it out myself, so thanks for the time save."

That put sheepish looks on the entire party. "Yeah, we were in your shoes and, well, we try and help where we can."

Mathew asked, "When is your first delve?"

"Tomorrow at 11:00 a.m."

Melinda jealousy said, "Ugh, lucky. Our Tier 1 was at 4:00 a.m., and I hated waking up that early. You got lucky coming during the off season."

"If you eat around 6:00 p.m., find us at the dining hall, that's when we'll be there, and we'd be happy to talk to you about the Tier 1 rift. You know, share our experiences."

Matt was touched. It was far more than strangers had to do after bumping into him and happening to share a name with one of them.

"I'll take you up on that offer, though I don't know if I'll make it tonight. I need to practice my skill and break in the new gear."

The older Mathew looked like someone had kicked his puppy until the other girl of the party, Matt thought she was introduced as Sam, said, "Then take our notes about the Tier 1 rift. It's nothing the official information doesn't have, but they have good tidbits about what we figured out that worked for us."

"There's an official guide?"

Melinda asked, "Didn't you get one when you checked in? With the check-in classes? Who was your guide?"

When Matt said Griff, they all winced. Obviously, they had also been subjected to his baby craze.

"Well, that explains it. If you see him, run the other way. We got stuck looking at baby pictures for like three hours once." The entire group shuddered at Melinda's statement.

"Yeah, well, now that you're on the PlayPen, there is a local network that has a bunch of good information. From guides on all the rifts to a ton of general information about Tiers. It's a mini-EmpireNet in a sense," she added with a shrug.

"Well, I'm glad I ran into you guys. Thanks. Who knows when I would have found that on my own? So, what's your party's name?"

That was the wrong thing to ask. Everyone but Melinda immediately started bickering. With a strained smile, she said, "We're still deciding." She pulled out her pad. "Let me send you our notes, and then I have to settle this."

He quickly got the file and escaped the conversation turning into a bigger argument with every new word added.

Matt went to the desk Melinda had pointed out and was led to a testing room by the receptionist. Once the

door was closed, he pulled the room's testing options upon his pad and selected 'Defensive - Full Evaluation,' The prompt stated the room would stop before he was injured, and it would give him a detailed breakdown on the skill's capacities.

Test settings prepared, and with great anticipation, Matt directed mana into the skill structure resting in his spirit.

At once, his reflection along the wall was wrapped in a mist-like covering. [Cracked Phantom Armor] was an opaque grayish silver with a tint of the blue of mana. It was vaguely shaped like full plate armor.

Searching, he couldn't find any gaps where normal joints would be. The skill covered everything, including his face, although he could see and breathe as though there was nothing in the way.

As Matt moved about and stretched, [Cracked Phantom Armor] didn't restrict him in any way, nor did it seem to weigh anything. So far, it was a perfect armor, with all the advantages of plate's coverage and none of the added weight or restricted movements.

With building nerves, Matt initiated the testing.

A flat voice called out, "Please, hold still. Defensive skill test engaging." A bladed arm extended from the ceiling and proceeded to swipe at Matt's chest. The strikes started feather-light and slowly increased in force until Matt was afraid it would pierce [Cracked Phantom Armor] and carve him up. He could actually feel the skills structure in his spirit destabilize as the hits grew in strength.

When Matt was about to stop the test, finally, the blade pierced the misty armor and was retracted before it could touch him.

"Physical slash testing complete. Analyzing results... Results determined. Skill will protect up to low Tier 2 slashing attacks. Any attacks that break through will have damage reduced by that flat rate. Please, increase mastery with skill or increase mana expenditure to increase the effect."

Matt was elated. One mana a second was a lot of mana for his Tier, and it showed he would be near-invincible in the Tier 1 rift. Even better, the Tier 2 rift would only be half as dangerous.

Talk about an amazing advantage.

His shit-eating grin froze as the flat voice announced, "Proceeding with piercing test."

For the next twenty minutes, Matt was poked, smashed, set on fire, frozen, electrocuted and, finally, even attacked with void.

The last one terrified him. Void was the most destructive known affinity, cutting through defenses at its Tier like they didn't exist. Matt was delighted to learn that [Cracked Phantom Armor] was slightly resistant to the element. While it wasn't immune, it outperformed any Tier 1 defenses not specialized in defending against the type. To his shock, the armor was nearly impervious against attacks composed of pure un-aspected mana, though a strong enough strike could still destabilize the armor and pierced through with force alone.

[Cracked Phantom Armor] was everything Matt hoped for and more. The original [Phantom Armor] was a stored skill meant as a life-saving measure, and its conversion into a channeling skill was just as resistant but permanently active.

Matt was happy he had chosen to take the risk and swipe the skill shard. Even if he didn't get more mana

at Tier 3, he would still be able to improve his mastery with the skill and, therefore, its effectiveness. It would be a slow process, but he could put in the hard work.

Feeling like he was floating on air, Matt went to the training room and sparred with the training aids until almost 9:00 p.m. With [Cracked Phantom Armor] active, he was able to trade blow for blow with the Tier 2 training aid. What would have been deep cuts were turned into light scratches and bruises instead of broken bones.

He felt like a new man.

While eating, Matt reviewed the information Melinda had sent him. With that and the official guide, he felt ready for tomorrow.

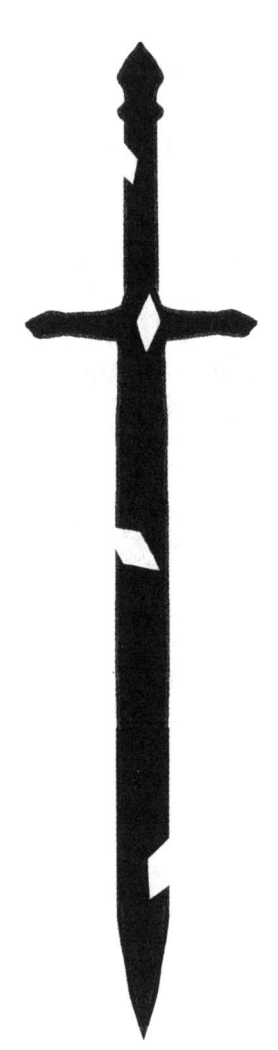

Chapter 5

Matt stood in front of the rift and just stared at it. It was a jagged tear in the fabric of reality, at least to his spiritual sense. It was only a slight shimmer to his physical senses, like a multi-colored heat haze.

Wrongness, hate, and discontent screamed back at him. He wasn't sure if that was what everyone felt, or if it stemmed from his loathing of the things that ravaged his city and slaughtered his parents.

The rift was enclosed in a building with three guards, two melee and one ranged fighter ready for a rift break. It was redundant. This rift was delved so often it needed extra mana added to it just to keep it from dissipating.

At least the Empire has more sense than the Junipers.

Matt pushed thoughts of the local nobles who ruled Lilly out of his mind. He drew his sword off his back and braced himself.

His slot of the rift time had just started, and he needed to move before he messed up the schedule for rift instances. Every fifteen minutes after someone entered the rift, there was a new instance made, which was completely independent of the others. If he waited too long, he could mess up the entire rotation for the day. Once the rift cycled, that instance could only be exited and never entered.

The guards didn't rush him, thankfully. After a deep settling breath, he walked into and through the rift.

The world bent and blurred for an instant, then snapped back to normal. Except now he was in the rift, standing near the wall of an underground cavern, exactly where the guide said he would be.

This was essentially a safe room in the rift. No monster would appear unless led by someone. Matt took stock of his surroundings, the ceiling was fifteen feet tall at his best guess, and lit torches lined the wall, providing light.

All was as it should be.

Looking behind him, Matt saw the rift portal shimmering. His escape if the monsters proved too difficult for him to handle.

Perfect.

Activating [Cracked Phantom Armor] Matt stepped into the adjacent room. The feeling of mana coursing through the skill's structure in his spirit was an odd but invigorating sensation. It felt like water rushing through a pipe, except it was inside of his spirit.

One lone goblin waited for him, right where the guide said it would be. Matt had decided to take his time on this fight, test his limits and those of the goblins.

When he crossed the threshold, the goblin charged with a shriek and wildly swung the bone shank in its hand. Sidestepping the wild and uncontrolled attack,

Matt had to stop from slashing down at the passing goblin and ending the fight instantly.

Letting the goblin swing repeatedly, Matt got a feeling for its speed and agility. Both would be good baselines for the entire rift. He pegged the monster at about four feet tall if it wasn't hunched so badly. The green humanoid creature only wore a ragged loincloth and wielded a pointy bone with a bit of leather wrapping the handle.

Matt let the next blow land on his left forearm, testing his skill, the monster's power and weapon. The bone fractured on [Cracked Phantom Armor], which left the goblin stumped for a heartbeat until it lunged with clawed hands outstretched.

Dodging to the side again, he swung at the goblin's waist. He expected to severely injure the monster in the first swing, then finish it on a second backswing, but the goblin was bisected by the attack.

Matt stepped back, dodging the blood and entrails which splattered the floor. Using his sword to push through the viscera, he saw the goblin's bones were thin, far weaker than a human at that size would have. More reminiscent of bird bones than human ones.

After the kill, he felt a small amount of essence trickle into the band on his wrist, and then into his spirit, waiting to be assimilated and distributed. It wasn't much, but it was progress. After the last year of only being able to train physically a few hours a day and working brutal hours, he was advancing.

Matt proceeded to the next room, where three goblins stood mindlessly until he crossed the threshold. From what he read, this was a characteristic of Tier 2 and below rifts only. As a rift's Tier increased, the realms became larger and the monsters more natural. A Tier 5 goblin rift would have had the entire clan attacking and retreating with strategy and cunning.

At Tier 1, these goblins just charged mindlessly. Matt still took the time to dodge and dispatched the closest monster with a slash. He cut deeply into its chest. The remaining two jumped at him and, with a heavy crosscut, Matt made two more corpses.

The next room contained five of the goblins, but they proved no greater challenge for their increased numbers. Unable to break his armor skill, they were easily crippled with even glancing blows.

Passing into the fifth room of the rift, Matt saw this goblin stood straighter and had an actual iron dagger. Though for its size, it was closer to a shortsword. Repeating his test of the first goblin, Matt determined the monster was no faster or stronger just better armed.

The soft iron dagger was noticeably misshapen where it hit [Cracked Phantom Armor], but the iron was useful to the outside, so Matt placed it in a separate bag for collecting loot. These small pieces of iron weaponry and the armor on the last monster were the only things of value this low Tiered rift had to offer.

With the same repeating pattern of one, three, then five goblins. The first three sets of rooms offered no challenge to Matt. The only improvement the third set had was they wore clothes not quite thick enough to call armor.

On the fourth set of goblins, Matt got his first challenge. This single goblin was a bit faster, no longer hunched, and of a slightly heavier build. It was also not as mindlessly aggressive as Matt tested it. To his relief, he discovered it wasn't trained just better with its decision making.

The room with five of that type of goblins got bloody. Matt was flanked by the little green monsters, and while his reach and reflexes were still better than the monsters, it took effort to kill them without being hurt. It was the first time Matt felt his swordsmanship abilities pushed inside the rift.

Two of the three that came straight on were taken out easily, but Matt had to deflect the last's dagger, stepping in and kneeing the goblin in the chest and sending it stumbling back. Matt was fighting as if the [Cracked Phantom Armor] wasn't active, treating every swing as a possible threat. He didn't want to get too reliant on the skill and let his longsword skills rust.

The final two that attempted to flank him were easy to take out. The left with a thrust as it lunged, and the right goblin with a slash that took off its outstretched arm as he backstepped.

Matt finished the goblins off before collecting the essence and loot.

Taking a drink of water, Matt pondered on [Cracked Phantom Armor]. It was permeable to the air, his clothes, and backpack while also stopping the goblin attacks completely. It didn't even have eye slits. He was just able to see through the mana construct perfectly as if it wasn't there.

It was amazing how a single skill turned this rift into a joke. He wasn't arrogant enough to imagine he could be this aggressive if he didn't have the skill to rely on, but when they couldn't even harm him, it was hard to treat the fights seriously.

Melinda's party's notes talked about how they got injuries the first few runs they did, and the increased

intelligence of the goblins made the backline take injuries despite the frontline's best efforts.

Even still, Matt hadn't taken a single blow he didn't *allow* to land. The rift monsters were smaller, weaker, and slower than him, which let him dictate the pace of combat.

He couldn't ignore the difference between Melinda's team and his solo delve. Without others to worry about, Matt didn't have the usually limited movement of melee fighters who couldn't dodge every blow because that would open the mages, archers, and supports to attack.

As he proceeded through the rift, he fought five more sets of goblins, collecting essence and iron weapons along the way. His sack was getting heavy to the point he placed it before the entrance of each room instead of carrying it with him.

An hour after he entered the rift, Matt arrived before the final room and peered in, careful not to cross the threshold. Five goblins in scale armor, just thumb-sized pieces of metal attached to long shirts, stood in front of a sixth, larger foe.

The final occupant of the room was a hobgoblin, 5'5" and bulkier than his lesser counterparts. It had actual plate armor, even though it was only iron, and had large gaps between the pieces.

This was one of three variations the final fight could be. It was also the most common, appearing around 50% of the time. The other two variations had a goblin mage and archer, respectively. Much harder fights because of the suppression the ranged fighters could put on a group.

Matt smiled, happy he didn't have to fight a variation his first delve. That would have been awful luck.

Stepping through the doorway, the five goblins charged in a loose formation, with the hobgoblin trailing behind and wielding an ax.

As the group approached, Matt circled left, so their formation was unable to flank him as easily. He lashed out at the first goblin to reach him and disarmed it. The goblin fell to the ground clutching at his stump.

One more obstacle in their way staggered the goblins out farther, so Matt had all of them dead or incapacitated by the time the hobgoblin approached. This was the fight he was anticipating.

The hobgoblin had a near-human size and with low Tier 2 strength and peak Tier 1 endurance and durability. Matt was not willing to underestimate this opponent. He had no one to help him if he messed up. With Tier 2 strength and a solid weapon, this hob could probably injure him, unlike his lesser cousins.

But this was what he'd trained for. He had spent months at Benny's practicing to solo a rift, and this was the time for him to prove it hadn't been time wasted.

Backing up while circling, Matt brought them back to the center of the room, where there were no bodies to foul up his footing, and stopped retreating. The hobgoblin continued his approach at the steady walk he had maintained the whole time and swung his two-handed ax when Matt stopped.

He backstepped, not trying to match the opponent's strength. As he went to lunge at the armored foe, using his straight weapon's ability to pierce armor, he had to jerk back as the hobgoblin reversed his swing and tried to impale him with the spike on the rear of his ax.

He used his aborted thrust to strike the handle of the ax, sending the weapon over his head while stepping

under and past the hob's arms. But he was unable to get a blow in as the hobgoblin retreated to the side and reset his stance.

For a moment, Matt and the hobgoblin locked eyes, then he surged forward with an overhead chop. The hob, thinking he had an easy victory, stepped back and let Matt's blow hit the ground before countering with a heavy, horizontal swing aimed at his neck.

Matt raised the pommel of his longsword and stepped to the opposite side of the swing, using the planted tip to block the heavy blow. Dropping the longsword after the block, Matt closed in with an elbow strike to its unarmored face that made the hob stumble as cartilage crunched.

With the head of the ax still near the floor, Matt kicked at the handle, ripping the weapon out of the hob's hands. Before the monster could recover, Matt drew his dagger from its thigh sheath under his armor and drove it up under the hob's chin and into its brain.

Shoving the hob back, Matt retreated until he stepped over his fallen longsword and, without taking his eyes off the still body of the hob, he picked his weapon up.

Watching the corpse, Matt waited until he felt the rush of essence to approach and ensure the goblins were dead. The essence he got from the hob was worth half of all the essence of the preceding rift.

Matt tried to steady his breath, but his heart hammered hard in his ears, proclaiming his triumph.

It had been an exhilarating fight. The hobgoblin had been smart and more experienced than any of the goblins preceding it. It also didn't have the mindless aggression that made the goblins easy to predict.

Closing his eyes and taking a deep breath, Matt pushed the energy down. The adrenaline was still pumping through his veins, and the accumulated essence created a rush Matt had never experienced before. His spirit felt heavy and full for the first time in his life.

He wanted more. He wanted to exit, then enter the rift again.

After a few deep breaths, Matt settled his emotions, though his racing heart wasn't slowing. Running a catalog of what he needed to do, he grabbed his sack of loot from the entrance and stripped the goblins and the hobgoblin of their armor and weapons.

With that taken care of, he turned his attention to the real prize of the rift. The reward for killing the strongest monster was always random and found in a distortion like the rift entrance. It could be anything from the most common of mana stones to the incredibly rare skill shards.

This being a low Tiered rift, it didn't often drop skill shards. According to the official guide, Tier 1 mana stones could appear in quantities ranging from one to one hundred, with the average being around seven.

Matt could hardly imagine making seven hundred credits for an hour and a half's work.

It makes all the hours at Benny's feel like wasted effort. I can make more in two hours delving the weakest of rifts than I made in a month.

This rift also could reward delvers with a few ingots of perfectly pure metals. Usually, only copper and iron, but there was the chance for steel or aluminum. The smiths prized these drops because they were easier to enchant when forging Tier 3 and above blades. Or at least the guide said so. Matt knew nothing about smithing or crafting skills.

The iron weapons he had collected along the way were just melted and sold as mundane building materials. The Empire paid for the scraps, believing there was no reason to have expensive mines ruining land for mundane metals when most low Tier rifts created them endlessly for free.

Matt approached the area of distortion next to the exit rift. It was a purple color to his spiritual sense. He wasn't sure if that was because of the item contained within or it was just random. The guide had said nothing about that.

After taking a deep breath and crossing his fingers for good luck, he sent a pulse of his mana at the small field. It shimmered before a small pile of stones appeared.

Mana stones. Jackpot.

Matt collected the small shards. They were only slightly bigger than the last knuckle on his pinky, in the shape of a hexagonal bipyramid, but thin. Each Tier 1 mana stone held 10 mana. Unlike artificial mana stones, once these were drained, they would turn to dust, and even the dust would disappear after a moment.

At each higher Tier, they held more mana at the same size, that being the reason a ten to one ratio was standard at the lower Tiers. Lower Tier mana stones didn't hold as much mana as the higher Tier did to equal the value. It was the convenience factor of having millions or billions of mana in a tiny stone that set their value greater than the mana in the stone. According to what he had read, the standard was set in the higher Tiers and calculated down.

Matt collected the small crystals and counted them from one hand to the other. Eight mana stones, one better than the average.

He couldn't stop smiling, eight hundred credits. 80 mana in his hands, the very power modern society needed to run was so small. So nondescript.

His instincts felt something this small should be fragile, even though Matt knew that was just an illusion from their resemblance to glass and size. The mana stones were nearly indestructible so long as they had mana remaining.

The only negative was if a mage wanted to convert the rifts mana stones to personal mana, there was a loss ratio of near 40%. It also took time and special equipment to slowly match the mage's unique mana signature before it could be safely absorbed.

That was why mana stones were mostly used for powering daily life and only occasionally used to refill mages, at great cost.

Matt pocketed the mana stones, stopped channeling mana to [Cracked Phantom Armor], then stepped through the portal, returning to the real world.

One of the guards waved Matt through to a check-out area where he could leave the iron scrap he collected.

The attendant looked like she was bored but trying to hide it. She almost succeeded. "Iron scraps can go on the scale, and if you are willing to report what you received, please do so."

Matt didn't mind. The Empire spent far more running this place than he had just earned. "Eight mana stones were the only reward. Well, besides the scrap." Matt waved at the sack full of metal.

"We are willing to purchase the mana stones here if you wish, or you can take it to any of the banks." The young lady sounded like she said these same words hundreds of times a day.

Come to think of it, she probably does.

Matt thanked her and walked away, checking his new account balance: 6,872 credits.

It was amazing and took a weight off his shoulders he hadn't realized was there. He wasn't sure what he wanted to do with it. He wasn't in a hurry to pay the credit card off as he didn't accrue interest being on The Path.

When he arrived back at the populated part of the island, he saw it was just after 12:30 and decided to go shower and eat lunch. After eating, Matt didn't know what to do. He couldn't remember a time where he didn't have *something* on his to-do list. At Benny's, he was working or training. Even at the orphanage, he was in lessons or doing extra training.

Matt was at a loss.

He decided to wander the island. It was little more than ten miles across.

It must have something I can do.

What Matt found during his walk was people at the beach. It seemed to be the way to relax as parties lounged in the sand or water and larger groups formed around various sports and games. He thought about joining but decided he was still too keyed up from the fight.

That led him to the interior of the island. He had checked, and there were no predators on the manmade island, so when he found a small clearing off one of the paths, he just laid down in the shade.

He found watching the slight breeze change the patterns of the shade cast by the trees was relaxing. For the first time since the alarms went off when he was eight, Matt allowed himself to fully relax.

Sometime later, he drifted off.

Matt woke slowly, stretching as he did. He felt good, light. So many worries were removed after getting a skill and a source of income.

Checking his pad, he hurried to the dining hall. Melinda's group said they'd meet him there, and he was eager to talk to someone about his delve.

Arriving only a little past six, Matt saw the group in line and waved at them as he joined the back of the line.

As he took his tray to their table, Matt saw the anticipation on their faces. Before he could fully sit down, Mathew asked, "So, how was it? You're still in one piece at least."

Melinda elbowed the other Mathew. "At least wait for him to sit down."

As soon as Matt had situated himself, she blurted, "So, how did it go? Don't keep us waiting. I didn't think to exchange numbers, so we couldn't call you when we got out of our rift."

"Yeah, I wanted to ask how your rift went first."

He was cut off with a series of 'nooos' and 'you firsts.'

Matt acquiesced and recounted his delve. "It wasn't bad. Your notes and the official information made sure there were no surprises. My Tier 1 Talent and skill synergize *really* well, and that made it so none of the regular goblins were able to hurt me."

As he spoke, he realized how weird that sounded. He was so used to thinking about his Talent in a negative light that he couldn't quite believe what he was saying.

"I took the fights seriously but, in the end, the goblins are so weak it was easy to not get hit at all."

Sam asked as soon as she could, barely getting her words out before the others, "What boss did you get? Did you pull a variant?"

"Nope. Just the standard, a solo hobgo—»

"Uh, how did you solo him? We all did, but not until we were peak Tier 1s and everyone else was ready to help," Kyle cut in this time.

The comment about peak Tier 1 jolted Matt. He hadn't cultivated his accumulated essence. He'd taken a *nap* instead.

"Oh no, I forgot to cultivate." Matt went to stand, but Vinnie, who he sat next to, dragged him back down.

"Chill, man. It's fine. You won't start to lose the accumulated essence for a few days. Relax. Really, man."

Matt sat back down reluctantly. "I feel so dumb. How did I forget the entire purpose of delving?"

"Yeah, how did you?" Vinnie had a smirk on his face as he asked, but it didn't come across as unkind.

"I got excited about the mana stones and how much they sell for. And ugh...took a nap in the woods." Matt blushed slightly as he said it.

When he didn't hear laughter from the others, he glanced around. They were blushing harder than him.

With red cheeks, Melinda raised her cup. "Here's to growing up poor and fixating on the money."

Everyone, including Matt, drank to that.

Matt broke the silence after that. He wanted to follow up on that statement. "I grew up in an orphanage after a rift break. What about y'all?"

That seemed to ruin the mood even more. It was Mathew who answered this time, "Same with us, and a lot of the sponsored folk here. The Junipers haven't been doing their damn job, and rift breaks are at an all-time high. They should be..."

Before Mathew could continue, Melinda covered his mouth. "Yes, we were orphaned as well, but talking bad about the nobility isn't smart without the power to defend yourself. *DO NOT* get us all in trouble, Mathew."

That finally stopped Mathew's struggles. Sam said, "My evasion instructor said he heard rumors the issue was being passed up."

Mathew scoffed around Melinda's covering hand. "That means we'll see results in twenty years if we are lucky. All the nobility are above Tier 15, and immortality makes bureaucracy take forever."

"Enough. We can't do anything. Matt, you were talking about the hobgoblin. How did it go?" Melinda forcefully changed the subject, and Matt took the topic shift willingly.

"It wasn't a long fight, honestly. While he was a better fighter than the goblins, he wasn't that good." Matt described his fight in detail, and everyone oohed and aahed at all the appropriate parts.

"What about you guys? How was your delve? And what do you do on your off days? I haven't had free time in forever."

Melinda said with a bright smile, "Our rift was easy. We're nearing the peak of Tier 2 and, in the next month or so, will advance, but we are balancing out our essence so we can advance together. And our days off. We usually spend the remaining time after the rift day cultivating. That usually takes up most of that day, but we have a strict no work policy on delve days.

"Hmm, the day after for us is training, both group and solo. We've all hired combat instructors for personal lessons. It's good, and when you can afford it, you should look into it. They are all Tier 7 or higher. Most are here on extended R&R. Either someone in their party got so injured they can't delve safely and are waiting for the cooldown on healings. Or they are taking a break from delving. They are all vetted and know their chosen fields."

That piqued Matt's interest. "Cooldown on healing? What is that? I thought you were just healed and back to normal. Just do it and be done. All better."

The entire group looked to Melinda this time. "Well, for small injuries, that's exactly how it works. But if you get ripped in half, regrowing and acclimating to the new parts takes time. Think of it like stress that accumulates. I don't want this to be a lecture, but I'm assuming you don't know how healing *actually* works, do you?"

At Matt's confirmation, she continued, "Don't feel bad. None of us knew either till I got a healing Talent. There are two types of healing spells. One is undirected. Cast the spell, and it does its thing. Each individual spell will be better at different things, but it just heals. The problem is, if you get a limb chopped off and you only have a basic healing spell, it will just seal the wound. It's technically healed.

"You need other spells, like [Regrowth] or [Regeneration] to heal missing limbs automatically, though [Regeneration] is a self-cast spell. The point is,

they will save your life but are kinda limited in their execution.

"The other type is a directed heal. It's like..." Melinda paused and pursed her lips before continuing slowly, "The best way to describe it is if someone gets their head chopped off, an undirected heal won't do anything. The spell will just consider them 'dead,' despite the fact you don't instantly die with decapitation. Even mundane medical technology can reattach a head.

"A directed healing skill is able to reattach a head, it just takes dozens of times more mana and absurd amounts of control and knowledge of anatomy. The spell doesn't guide you if you mess up. You just killed somebody while trying to save them."

Mathew continued for her, "I like to think it's like patching a blanket; a hole can just be stitched together, and a directed healing spell can easily do that, but a blanket that was ripped in half is harder to get back together."

Melinda smiled at him. "We got distracted. The point is, after a lot of healing, the body needs time to recover or the next healing will be even harder and might not take, so parties wait, and that gives PlayPens combat trainers. The higher the Tier someone is, the longer the cooldown can be for the same injury."

"The day before a rift, we attend classes: math, science, and pursue a crafting hobby. Do some group training at some point. It's the recommended schedule, but you can flip the days if you want."

Tara spoke up, "The night after a delve is for partying. There are clubs and parties every night, but most only go after a delve to blow off steam, which is where we are going next. You will come, right? Let us show you the scene."

Kyle chimed in, "Yeah, you don't have to stay long, just have a drink or two, play some pool with us, and then you can head home. It's too late to cultivate anyway. Better to wait till morning when you can do it properly."

Matt wanted to decline. He felt the urge to rush back to his room and cultivate. The pleading looks they gave him finally decided for Matt.

"Sure, I'll go, but just for a little while."

Matt and Kyle played doubles pool and had their collective asses handed to them by Sam and Tara. Mostly Tara.

"It's still unfair your archery sense works for all projectiles. It's cheating, Tara," Kyle whined, and Matt agreed.

The archer girl was even using her non-dominant hand, and they had limited her to two shots per round, but she was still clearing the table.

Her skill felt superhuman, and it was. Talents were unique and wondrous. From what Matt understood, Tara had a projectile sense of some type. Talents weren't commonly shared except with the closet of friends or spouses. There was too much that could be gleaned and countered when the ins and outs of a Talent were known.

If her Talent alone makes her this good at pool, just how good is she with a bow?

Melinda and Mathew snuggled together in a dark corner, while Vinnie disappeared with a woman he'd met.

Matt nodded toward the entwined healer and tank. "So, they're together, then?"

Sam tiredly shook her head in response.

Kyle translated that into words. "Nope. Our sponsor *heavily* suggested we avoid any relationships in the team until after Tier 5. It wasn't quite an order, but Melinda and Mathew would jump off a cliff if Harper asked them to."

Tara scoffed. "Like you wouldn't?"

"True." Kyle tipped his beer at his teammate.

Matt understood. If Dena or Eric had 'heavily suggested' something, he would have taken it as an order as well.

"Did he give any reasons?"

"Yeah, he saw how Melinda and Mathew looked at each other. He said the risk of young love not working was pretty high, and youthful mistakes could break up a young couple in a flash. That would destroy our team. So, they're waiting." Kyle missed his shot while answering.

"I was meaning to ask. How does being sponsored as a team work?"

"Pretty much the same as a solo, but we can't add more people to the team without our sponsor's approval. Other than that, nothing really different." Tara flopped backward onto the pool table, beer forgotten to the side. "How did you get picked by a sponsor, Matt? Were you top of the class or something fancy like that?"

Matt hesitated to share his failure, but he got the feeling they were honest and kind, so he decided to share a little. "No. Our orphanage was so overcrowded we all got Awakened at thirteen and pushed out."

All three winced. "It wouldn't have been that bad. They did what they could to ensure we got some face time with guilds and corporations even before going to the Awakening Center. I almost got recruited to a guild, but my Tier 1 Talent is—"

Sam chimed in, "You don't have to say more."

"Nah, it's okay. My Talent is…limiting. Yeah, 'limiting' is the best word for it. It really restricts my cultivation, and that broke my provisional contract. Luckily, the recruiter was a good guy and helped me find a way forward. I just needed to make money, then buy a delve slot. So, I got a shitty job at a shitty inn. Worked there for over a year, then Dena and Eric walked in."

Matt had their attention now. "They were Tier 5s and stronger than anyone I'd ever met at the time. But they were kind." He gave them a look. "I'm sure you know how high Tiered people can be."

Tara and Sam simply nodded. A dark look flashed across Kyle's face.

Receiving murmurs of agreement, he continued, "I was working twelve-hour days as a general handyman, with only some time before everyone else woke up to practice. So that's when I did it. After they checked in, they came down to spar roughly the same time I did.

"Dena asked for a sparring partner while she worked on her staff technique, and that's pretty much how the next month went. They sparred with me in the mornings. Later, they said I had good talent and they felt my Tier 3 would pair with my Tier 1, fixing my problems.

"So, they had me spar with Dena at low Tier 3 strength." At the sound of three intakes of air, Matt paused. He reminisced over the fight. "It wasn't even close. She was so much faster and stronger, I was barely able to eke out a tiny little scratch. But it was enough.

"They said hitting a Tier 3 at Tier 1 was special enough that they'd sponsor me. Though I didn't know what that really entailed. A few hours later, I was on a train headed here. Shit, that was only last week."

"Wow. If we didn't have a rule against sleeping with friends, I'd drag you to my room right now." Tara's words made Matt blush a bit before everyone laughed. She'd even bounced her eyebrows, cutting the tension of the story with a joke.

"What about you guys?"

Sam piped up, "We were all friends in school when the rift break happened. It was bad." She took a long pull from her bottle before continuing. "We were close to the initial hit area, out at the edge of town. Our teacher died killing the giant kobold that pushed through the door. That turned out to be a blessing. Their bodies mostly blocked the door, and only small monsters could just barely squeeze through."

At that point, their gazes turned to Mathew and Melinda in the corner. "Mathew took charge and got everyone to pile stuff in front of the door to block the entrance off more. Took a blow doing it that nearly shredded his back. I still remember Melinda holding bloody rags to his wounds, crying. I know there isn't any way to predict Talents but, at that moment, I knew she would be a healer. Talent or not.

"Out of the twenty-three kids in our class, we were the only ones who lost everyone. The others had someone left to go to. But not us. That made us close. We've been inseparable since. When our Awakening's happened, we all got pretty lucky, nothing detrimental."

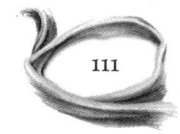

Tara winced. "Sorry, Matt, I didn't mean—"

"It's fine. Really. It happens to some. And that 'some' includes me."

Clearing her throat, Sam finished the story. "We'd already decided to team up. From day one really. So, we had spent the entire time training together. The problem was Melinda."

Matt peeked over at the blonde, giggling into Mathew's shoulder. *How was she a problem?*

Catching his glance, Sam explained, "Yeah, Melinda's Tier 1 Talent was rated as 'exceptional' in the healing category. It made a massive stir."

"Fucking shit show is more like it," Kyle grumbled.

"Yeah. Well, everyone came. It was overwhelming. There were hundreds of guilds and groups offering to pay massive bonuses to attract her. Our sponsor heard about it, and seeing how they were acting, put a stop to it.

"Harper's a Tier 7, and he was like a walking storm. His very presence made everyone scurry back to the holes they crawled out of." Her disgust was palpable in the scowl that crossed her face.

"Harper tried to take Melinda aside, but she refused to let go of Mathew and Tara. Literally. She was hanging onto their clothes. So, Harper herded us all to an empty room and explained what was going on. Apparently, there is something of a finder's fee for low Tier guilds to get rare Talents for higher Tier guilds or noble families," Sam said.

Kyle added, "They recruit them with long, nearly unbreakable contracts and then basically sell them to the highest bidder. The guilds were trying to turn Melinda into a cash cow."

Tara took back over, "Harper gave us EmpireNet access, and everything he said was true. The Empire doesn't technically allow it, but it's really hard to police on low Tiered worlds. The guilds can easily get away with it when the local nobles don't care enough."

Apparently seeing Matt's expression morph, Kyle quickly added, "Not that the people are treated badly, it's just they don't get a say on where they go. Their services are essentially leased out by the guild. But, sometimes, it's the only way off these planets."

Tara wrapped up, "So, Harper offered to sponsor us if we could meet his standards. A 'basic competency test' he called it."

They all shuddered at that. "It was a very tough few months, but we're better for it."

A thought popped up in Matt's mind, and he vocalized it. "Why has everyone been so friendly here? Not that I mind, but it seems odd."

"Easy answer is 90% of the people on the PlayPen this time of year are sponsees. Most of us come from poor backgrounds, and now we're hot shit. In, oh, I don't know, maybe four or five months, we'll have another wave of newbies roll in. Most of those will be the rich kids here to spend mommy and daddy's money and die. There's like a 10% to 25% death rate amongst the non-sponsored, but they spend money like crazy. That's why the Empire gives spots to people running the cities. The politicians pass them off as favors, and the rich help pay for the rest of us. It also lets the rich kids possibly show off some skill and maybe get sponsors of their own."

Matt looked aghast.

How do people die in that rift?

Seeming to read his face, Kyle answered, "The non-sponsored kids don't get the discounts or anything, but they don't have restrictions either. So, they get cocky and throw themselves into the Tier 2 and 3 rifts *way too early*. Then they die."

Tara chimed in, "Going back to the original question, you never know who's going to be a powerhouse in the future. It could be anyone here. Besides, we aren't competing for spots on The Path or anything. We're all already on it. The higher everyone climbs, the better. No reason to cut each other down."

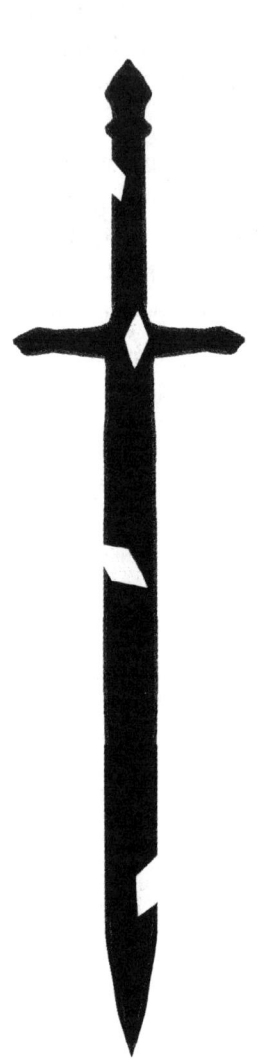

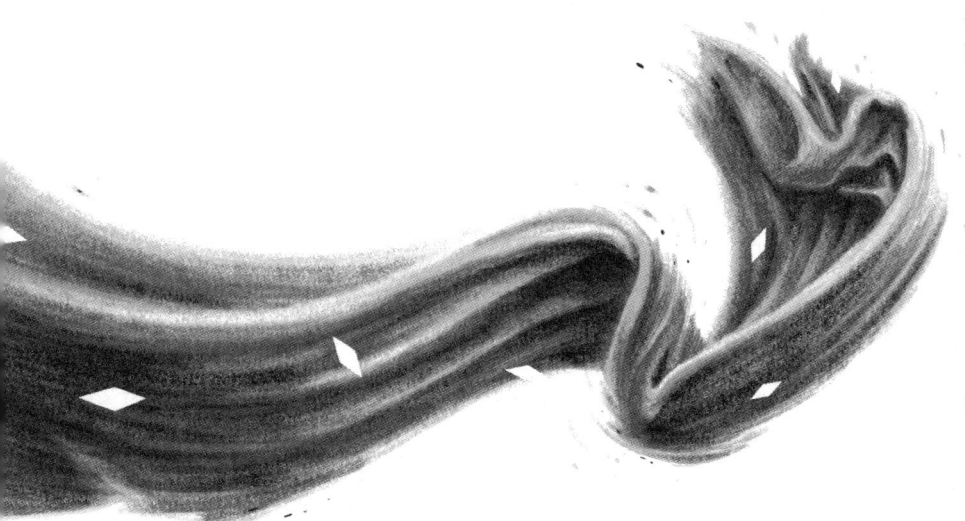

Chapter 6

The next morning, Matt got up and reviewed the cultivation guide he read last night. There wasn't anything complicated to do at Tier 1. He just had to relax and focus on his essence.

As excited as Matt was, he couldn't relax enough to reach the required state to cultivate. He tried sitting, legs crossed, sitting in a chair, even tried slow movements. None of the top-recommended positions worked for him. Eventually, he flopped onto his bed and was slowly able to get a good grip on his essence.

The essence he had accumulated delving sat in his spirit, concentrated in the center but also present dispersed through the rest of the sphere.

Once Matt had a good mental grasp on the essence, he felt two paths. One led to his body, and that channel was open and seemingly thirsty for essence. The other led to what he knew was his mana side but felt completely

sealed off. No matter how he tried, the essence couldn't go down that side.

Matt hadn't *actually* believed it would work, but it had been worth an attempt. Giving up, he sent the essence to the physical side.

That was all there was to it. There was no real effort to cultivation, just concentration and time. He had to constantly coax the essence along or it would try and settle stagnant in his spirit, but that was all.

He found it incredibly boring.

What felt like minutes later, Matt was finished, his spirit empty of essence. He looked at his pad and saw it was almost 3:00 p.m. He had started at just after 7:00 a.m.

Where did eight hours go?

Matt felt robbed and hungry upon seeing the time. Sighing, he changed into sparring clothes and quickly ate a light lunch before heading to the training room.

He did what Melinda's group suggested last night. For one thousand credits, he could purchase a simulation of the final room of the Tier 1 rift. It even came with the variations.

Matt made the purchase and wandered, looking for an open training room, but he didn't find one until the fourth floor. Linking his pad and simulation to the room, Matt activated [Cracked Phantom Armor].

Six training aids came out, and he exchanged blows with the aids.

After a few hours of practicing and learning the aids' patterns and strategies, Matt went and had dinner with Melinda and company. They had a tactics training class after dinner, so they didn't linger long.

Matt went back to his room and browsed the available classes. Everything seemed useful, but he had to prioritize

at least a little. It was only recommended to take one or two classes at a time, and with them meeting once every three days, they were built around the three-day delve schedule.

First, he looked up the finances class Dena had recommended. Most classes lasted two months, and he was in the middle of a cycle, so he'd be waiting no matter which classes he chose, but he wanted to browse. The other one he decided on was manners & etiquette, a recommendation passed on by Melinda's group's sponsor to them.

After having that planned out, he looked up the personal trainers.

Matt stood in front of the rift again. It shimmered with colors he couldn't put names to. Rift really was an apt name. With a bracing breath, he stepped through.

The beginning of the rift was the same as it had been three days ago. The entire rift was a repeat of the last delve. That was until the final room, where he only saw four goblins in the scale armor. To the side, he found the fifth.

It was an archer. Matt didn't have anything to fear from this goblin as it was only mid-Tier 1 in strength, and its bow wasn't particularly powerful.

Still, Matt went over the scenarios that had worked for this combination yesterday.

Stepping through, Matt ran at the four charging goblins, veering off to the right-most goblin and stabbing his longsword through the small monster while charging at the goblin with the bow.

Using its comrade as a meat shield, Matt closed the distance before the others could rescue the archer, who stood shooting arrows into the corpse on Matt's blade for a breath too long.

That mistake let Matt add one more to his goblin shish kebab. Turning while using his foot to push the goblins off his blade he lashed out at the hobgoblin, who had nearly reached his back as it was closer to the rear when Matt ran past the group of monsters.

Matt's attack caused the hobgoblin to step back, aborting its swing. That change in location caused the goblin charging past to catch the ax in the side.

The final two goblins flanked Matt to either side, trying to box him in and restrict his movement. He stepped to the right, parrying the goblin's swing before stepping on its feet and hip-checking the smaller creature.

The force sent the goblin falling backwards, but Matt standing on its feet caused the monster's weak ankle bones to snap.

With a stomp, he finished the goblin off while keeping an eye on the hob and remaining goblin.

The goblin ran out wide left of the hob and refused to move closer to Matt than the hob did. It was probably the best move the creature could make at this point, and it stood by, covering the hobgoblin's weak side.

Matt tried baiting out the goblin, but it refused to wet his blade like its brothers did. With the weaker goblin's assistance, Matt was forced to retreat from the heavy blows of the hob's ax.

Biding his time, Matt waited for his opportunity. When the hobgoblin struck out, Matt didn't dodge or deflect the strike but, instead, blocked the haft of the weapon with the flat of his longsword.

Matt took advantage of the opening and ran his blade down the haft to catch the hobgoblin's unprotected fingers.

Flesh met steel and lost.

Screeching in pain, the hob retreated, unable to hold his weapon. Matt used that opportunity to finish off the goblin next to the hob with a clean cut.

Seeing the hob was just clutching its mangled hand, he thrust through the unprotected arm opening in the plate, bisecting the last remaining monster.

Looking around, Matt felt like this could have been done cleaner. He might not have been hit, but that didn't feel like a particularly high bar to set with opponents this weak.

There is a reason this rift was kept when they made the PlayPen.

Sighing, he collected the bloody armor and weapons before moving to the reward distortion.

Sweeping it with his spiritual sense, he felt it was an orange color this time. But not quite. It had a multicolored thread weaving through the field.

Matt wasn't sure if it meant anything but waited until the thread was at its most visible pulse before dispelling the field.

There were two bars of metal. He thought they were steel but wasn't sure. He wasn't a smith, after all.

It was something to look into, and a class on blacksmithing would be useful for identifying materials like this. At least then he would be able to tell the quality of weapons apart.

The more he thought about it, the more he liked the idea. If he was going to be a mostly melee fighter, it would do him well to understand his weapons of choice better.

Matt exited the rift and sold the steel bars to the receptionist for five hundred credits apiece. The money added to his account etched a smile onto his face.

Overall, he felt it was a successful delve.

The next month and a half were some of the best in Matt's life. He delved, he cultivated and advanced, and he learned.

All while becoming closer to Melinda's group. Most of his days off were spent with them. After delve days, they all relaxed together, watched movies, played games, drank, or just explored the island. They also sparred together, which was a learning experience for Matt. They were strong and coordinated, never letting him get past Mathew or Kyle.

They never tried to hurt each other, but they had fun challenging one another in the controlled environment.

Over the time they spent together, they became true friends, and Matt was grateful. He hadn't let anyone get close at the orphanage or Benny's.

Matt didn't think he had purposely kept people away, just that he hadn't met people he wanted to become that

intimate with. Most of the people at Benny's were older and jaded from life, content to eke out enough to live but little more.

He wanted greatness. Melinda's group wanted the same. They pushed themselves and refused to languish at the lower Tiers.

The classes were interesting. The financing class was an eye-opener. Matt didn't realize he had misunderstood Dena's letter. When she had said the credit limit was twenty thousand, he had assumed she meant credits and based his purchases around that misconception.

He had been given a credit limit of twenty thousand Tier 1 mana stones not twenty thousand credits. It was a mind-boggling amount of money that Matt couldn't even imagine. It was an ungodly number of credits. That extra cash let him hire a Tier 7 melee trainer to give him lessons.

It was subsidized by the Empire, but he still had to pay fifty thousand credits. He had been hesitant to go into that much debt but, after the first lesson, he had no regrets.

Dominic was a 6'4" monster who mainly used a sword and shield but was competent in most weapons. After seeing Matt's skill, Dominic had him rotating weapons, with a focus on a shield and one-handed weapons. His reasoning was that if Matt ever joined a team, a shield was usually better for the group than a single longsword user.

It was challenging. He thought he was good with the longsword, and Dominic even confirmed he was. But when using a shield and sword, he felt clumsy and had a hard time getting into a groove that felt as natural as he did with his longsword.

After Dominic felt he was ready, he had Matt tackle the Tier 1 rift with the sword and shield. It was a different experience from his runs with a longsword. With a longsword in hand, he barely took half an hour to clear out the rift. With the shield and sword, it took almost two hours. There was an incremental improvement in each run, but not something Matt was satisfied with.

Dominic had even started Matt with spear training, with and without a shield. He was sure that would be his next weapon to take into the rift and delve with to get practical experience.

During his delves, Matt hadn't had exceptional luck, either good or bad, with the rift rewards. He mostly earned around the average of seven mana stone value either in metals or mana stones.

On the other hand, his cultivation was almost a quarter of the way through Tier 1. It was only that fast because he didn't have to split the essence. It was nice to advance quickly, but he was warned by everyone that the Tier 2 rift was a large step up in difficulty.

Once Matt broke through to Tier 2, he would see a larger improvement. While cultivating and distributing essence, a cultivator only got half the results and got the other half when he broke through the Tier barrier. It was the reason a new Tier 2 was so much stronger than a peak Tier 1.

Even so, Matt was seeing improvements in his strength, speed, and endurance. The changes weren't massive, but after every delve, he could fight a little longer, strike a little harder, and move just a bit faster.

He was cultivating after his delve when his pad chirped. He ignored it until the pad vibrated. He had it

set to 'do not disturb' and only an emergency contact would override that setting.

Matt rolled over and looked at the message after snatching up the pad.

Melinda sent a message, 'Have you seen the news? Come to our suite. Quick.'

A worried Matt hurried to their collection of rooms and found them in the common area watching the TV.

An official-looking man spoke to the screen. Behind him was an expensive-looking manor with people crawling over it like ants.

"...rise. The Empire expects its nobility to guide and protect the common people. After a thorough investigation, the Empire has found the Juniper family negligent to the extreme. With this verdict, the Empire will be sending relief efforts to repair all cities that have been affected by rift breaks."

Matt gasped. *That's* what this was about? Negligence from the nobility leading to widespread destruction, solely because they hadn't wanted to take measures to prevent it wasn't exactly news to him. He expected the news to be *another* rift break and city burned.

"Holy s—" Matt was hushed by everyone.

He squeezed in between Vinnie and Sam on the couch as the broadcast continued.

"Because of the devastation, there will be compensation to all affected parties. Please, be patient. Millions have lost loved ones and family members. The Emperor cannot bring them back, but reparations will be given to those remaining and punishment to those responsible."

A crowd behind the camera cheered at that. The official held up a hand, and it was instantly quiet. "By

the Emperor's will, all will be made as whole as possible. Healers, both mundane and magical, will be arriving on Lily in the next few months. This includes psychiatrists. Their services will be on an at need basis. All will get their time and help. Please, be patient."

He looked down at his pad for a moment, then back at the crowd and camera. "Standby for a royal decree from His Majesty, Emperor Emmanuel the Third. Hear and obey."

With a flick of his fingers from his pad to the camera, a new image replaced the official.

The man on the throne was tall and in seemingly simple clothes, but Matt was sure they probably cost more than twenty planets would generate in a decade.

The Emperor was dark-haired, with gold eyes that gave off a visible light like miniature flashlights. The odd part was it didn't interrupt the view of the man's eyes, which Matt could see clearly. He wasn't sure if it was how the Emperor looked in person or if it was a camera trick, but it gave a feeling of strength and power as though a single look moved mountains.

His voice was deep. Even through the recording, Matt felt the pressure on his chest like a physical weight. "It has come to our attention that the Barony of Juniper of planet Lilly is guilty of neglect to the extreme. We, after reviewing the events, have decided an outsider will care for the planet no more than any other noble family raised to the position.

"Our solution to this predicament is as follows. The Path of Ascension is meant to raise the strong, and from The Path, your next noble will be chosen.

"The first person or group who was affected by the rift breaks to reach Tier 15 will be given the opportunity

to take the noble title. It is our hope that someone who has experienced the tragedy of rift breaks will not take the lives of their subjects as lightly as the Junipers did." He then repeated himself with more enunciation. "*Any* who have been affected and are on The Path are eligible. Good luck."

With that, the image returned to the official. "The Emperor has spoken. The planet will be placed under an advisory council until one of your own ascends to the position. More information will be passed in the coming days."

The man stepped away, and the view of the reporter was spliced in and started chattering.

Matt and the rest looked at each other in shock.

"Holy shit," Tara said. That broke the shocked silence, and everyone clamored to talk. Eventually, it settled, but the excitement was still palpable.

Mathew, who had a quietly weeping Melinda in his arms, said, "I saw it myself, but I can't believe it. I thought it would take an official challenge to the noble family and killing them at Tier 15 to get revenge. Shit, I don—"

Melinda slapped his chest. "It's a good thing, dummy. Now we don't have to risk ourselves to right that wrong, and people are getting the support they deserve, not..." she hiccupped, interrupting herself, "not just revenge, but actual help."

Vinnie voiced Matt's growing fear, "Is this concern, or something else? The Emperor himself heard of this incident on a Tier 4 planet? There are how many thousands of planets below Tier 5 in the Empire? Why does he care? It seems too good to be true. And how did he even hear of this? To ascend, the Emperor must break

the Tier 50 barrier. He could break this planet in half. It doesn't sit right with me."

Sam chimed in, "I can't say how or why he stepped in, but he pissed a lot of people off with his decree, that's for sure. Normally, new baronies are given to the second and third children of higher nobles. Only the first child of a noble to hit the Tier for their rank can take the title. Everyone else gets nothing."

"In my in-depth nobility class, they talked about it. New lower Tier planets are always being added to the Empire and doing this sets a precedent that probably pissed a lot of higher nobles off. What plot can there be in that?"

The seven of them talked around the topic until dinner. They couldn't believe there was a chance that any one of them could be the next baron of this planet. Even if there were stronger people who had suffered the attacks and were on The Path, it was still The Path of Ascension, and anyone could fall off at any time.

After they finished eating, Melinda dropped even more shocking news. "Are you all ready to go to see our Tier 3 Talents?" Matt was shocked. They had said they were at peak Tier 2, but this was a huge step and the last Talent they would have unless they got to Tier 25, then Tier 50.

"Wait, you guys broke through? What are we waiting for? Let's go! This is huge." Matt was excited. This was their first step into the larger Empire. After reaching Tier 3, people could only spend six months at the PlayPen before they had to make their own way on The Path of Ascension.

They all looked at him with expressions he couldn't place. It wasn't the happiness he expected. The looks put his hackles up.

"Matt, we talked about it over the last few days and, well... Here, it's easier to see. Please, don't share this with anyone. Obviously, we trust you, and this will let you know we're okay when we leave."

His pad pinged, and he pulled it out to see...

> The party "Unbroken" has sent an offer of alliance.
> <u>Alliance Details:</u> Full viewing access to individual profiles granted to all members.

Matt's thinking ground to a halt. This was massive. It would let him see their skills and Talents. It was more than most friends shared, and a tremendous show of trust.

With only a moment's thought once his brain started working, he accepted and gave them the same permissions. He could trust them. Even if this bit him in the ass in the future, Matt was willing to risk it. They were friends.

He saw the group check their pads with relieved smiles until Mathew gasped, "What is this bullshit?"

The others had incredulous looks as well as they saw his Talent. Sam was the first to react to his skill. "What is this skill? It's broken. What are these resistance numbers? This is absurd."

Sheepishly, he said, "Just two useless things that synergize really well." He still wasn't used to thinking of his Talent as a positive.

"Hah. 'Really well' is an understatement, Matt. I wish our Mathew had tank skill that good." Mathew, who was next to Melinda, looked at her as she said that, gave an exaggerated shocked look, and clutched at his heart.

Matt took the time to look at their information.

Mathew:
- **Talent - Tier 1:** Everyone in the party has lowered threat generation. Threat generation is redirected to an individual of choice.
- **Talent - Tier 3:** Unknown. Please, visit a Talent scanner.
- **Skills:** None.

Melinda:
- **Talent - Tier 1:** All healing skills are 50% more effective and cost 50% less mana to cast.
- **Talent - Tier 3:** Unknown. Please, visit a Talent scanner.
- **Skills:** [Ranged Heal]

Kyle:
- **Talent - Tier 1:** All strength allocation has double the effect.
- **Talent - Tier 3:** Unknown. Please, visit a Talent scanner.
- **Skills:** None.

Samantha:
- **Talent - Tier 1:** Poisons and venoms only affect designated targets.
- **Talent - Tier 3:** Unknown. Please, visit a Talent scanner.
- **Skills:** [Venom Strike]

Vincent:
- **Talent - Tier 1:** Innate [Earth Manipulation].
- **Talent - Tier 3:** Unknown. Please, visit a Talent scanner.
- **Skills:** [Earth Manipulation]

Tara:
- **Talent - Tier 1:** Innate understanding of ranged weapons.
- **Talent - Tier 3:** Unknown. Please, visit a Talent scanner.
- **Skills:** None.

Matt's jaw dropped. None of their Talents were weak. Melinda had joked about Mathew not being a good tank, but redirecting threat generation meant enemies wouldn't prioritize the backline damage dealers and healers. That was a defensive frontline's entire job, and he could do it without an expensive skill shard.

Kyle could focus on other parts of physical cultivation with his Talent, and that would either let him get a bit more mana cultivation and be a true hybrid or be an even better physical cultivator. He could be twice as strong as anyone on his Tier while being better in the other aspects of physical cultivation, or even match someone a Tier above in pure strength.

Sam's Talent was what every poison mage dreamt of and would beg for any skill shard that would be able to mimic it. Most had to become solo delvers because, while they were immune to their own skills, they would kill their allies as quickly as their enemies.

Vinnie had [Earth Manipulation] as an innate skill, which meant it was a free core skill. Matt knew that skill. A Tier 10 on The Path had used it not five months ago in a tournament to beat every one of her opponents without moving a muscle.

She had stood there with arms crossed, and as soon as her opponents had touched the ground, it simply swallowed them. She had even faced an opponent who had a flight skill and had simply launched spears of stone at them until she impaled them.

Tara's innate understanding of ranged weapons was less flashy, but if it worked like other innate understandings Matt had heard of, she would need next to zero training to get decent with a ranged weapon. She'd need far less to master the weapon than any normal cultivator would. Matt had only read of single weapon understandings, never such a broad category covered by a Talent.

Then there was Melinda. Matt didn't know what to think. It was no wonder she had been given a rating of exceptional. From everything he'd read, 50% was the acknowledged limit of what a Talent could do to a skill or type of skill without giving something up in return. And she had *two* in one Talent.

Just having a talent with two abilities was already incredibly rare, but having two with maxed benefits? She might be the only one on the entire planet.

They were watching Matt as he took in the information. He just glared at them before turning up his nose and saying, "I hate all of you."

Matt paced outside of the row of testing rooms. It had taken half an hour of bickering about how broken the Talents of the others were before the stalling became obvious and the party faced their destiny.

He was more nervous than any of the group had seemed to be. He wasn't sure if it was just that they were hiding it better or truly not nervous. They may have hesitated in coming but, once they arrived, they didn't falter.

As he paced, he felt a breeze then, suddenly, there was Griff and a woman next to him.

Matt knew Griff was the second in command of the PlayPen and Tier 15. Judging by the way he stood at the woman's side but slightly behind her, Matt assumed she could only be the person running the PlayPen.

I'm pretty sure I remember reading it was always a Tier 20 in charge of a PlayPen. Why would a Tier 15 and a Tier 20 both show up?

Matt gulped. Had something gone wrong? Why were the two most powerful people on the island here? Then a second breeze alerted Matt to yet another presence.

He turned and saw the official from the earlier proclamation. The news reporters after his announcement said he was a Tier 30, and a high-ranking minister of the Empire who had the Emperor's trust.

Why are all these people here?

Matt felt the fear building at the unknown and quickly looked between the group of three and the doors. He wasn't dumb and could tell exactly what door they were viewing.

He wished he had brought his sword. It wouldn't have done any good against the three, but he couldn't let something happen and just stand by. Matt had promised himself long ago he wouldn't let the people he cared about to be snatched away from him.

Just as Griff noticed him and opened his mouth, the right-most door opened. The door they had been watching. Melinda came out pale, tired-looking, and covered in sweat.

That grabbed all their attention, and the official spoke up, "Miss—"

Melinda cut him off. "I know. Can we wait until my party is done? I don't want to have to do this twice."

A Tier 3 had just interrupted a Tier 30. Matt looked at the official, and while he looked like he wanted to argue, he said nothing.

Matt felt out of his depth.

Melinda looked to Matt, and that drew the attention of the three powerhouses. Griff spoke up, "Hey, Matt, maybe you should clear out. Okay?"

He was surprised the Tier 15 remembered him at all. As he was about to agree and leave, Melinda once again spoke up, "He's an ally of our party, so I'd like him to remain. Please?"

Once again, the others just agreed.

Matt was *really* concerned now, and he felt jittery as his mind raced through the possibilities. His flight or fight response was going haywire. All he could think about was helping Melinda and getting away from the immortals. His body screamed at him to do something, even though his mind knew either would be useless in the face of these powerhouses.

The only thing letting him keep a hold of himself was they weren't hostile. Clearly, they were here for Melinda, and considering what she had just been doing, there were only a few possibilities as to what could have drawn these people of position and power here.

Just what did her Talent reveal?

Matt could check but didn't feel comfortable reaching for his pad with the stillness in the hall. If he broke it, those three might just decide to act.

It only took another few minutes for the other five to come out and, as soon as Tara walked out of her room, they were ushered into a conference room down the hall.

The official started before they were even inside, "Miss Combs, we were all alerted to your Talent. We couldn't see what it is, but the rating came back as Exceptional: Unique, top priority. We would like to offe—"

A quick two beeps interrupted the man, and his face drained of blood. With shaking hands, he pulled his pad out and flicked a finger at the wall. For the second time that day, Matt saw the Emperor.

Matt gulped as the immortals went to one knee, heads bowed. He and Melinda's party followed suit a moment later.

"Your Majesty, what can your humble servants do for your excellency?"

Out of the corner of Matt's lowered head, he saw the official shaking slightly.

"Good, you got to them already. You three get out." There was a power in those words. Even with his face toward the ground, Matt felt it. He could *see* it. The world grew sharper, and colors gained contrast for an instant before returning to normal.

Matt didn't know what the Tier 50 did, but Griff and the other two looked pale and haggard after the words were spoken. He felt nothing where the other three clearly felt *something*.

Immediately, the official, Griff, and the woman were simply gone. Matt didn't even hear the door open or close.

Still kneeling, they waited for what came next.

"Get up, kids, will you? Ugh, this is a shit show."

As they stood and faced the Emperor, they saw him at a desk with pads scattered about and papers covering the free spaces. Screens obstructed part of the desk until a wave from the Emperor made them vanish.

"That's better. Hey, kids. Who would have thought I'd be hearing about Lilly twice in one day?" The Emperor smiled and waved at them. Matt felt his stomach tighten.

"I'll get right to it. These inter-planet connections are expensive, so I'll try to be brief. My AI just pinged me about your Talent, Melinda. Can I call you Melinda?"

Melinda just nodded, still struck dumb. The Emperor seemed surprisingly personable. During the royal decree,

he was stern and, even in a recording, he had an air around him that screamed power and authority.

Now, he was like a kind uncle. Even his luminescent eyes were warm. It unsettled Matt. In his experience, people with strength didn't take notice of the weak unless they had something they wanted.

"Thanks. I deal with enough formalities every day. Would you mind sharing why my AI lost its shit with notifications? You don't have to, but it might make things easier."

Melinda had to clear her throat twice before she could get any words out, "You can't just...umm...see it, Your Majesty?"

The Emperor chuckled at that. "Nope. If there is one loophole in the Talent AI, it risks security breaches, so not even I can see without permission being shared from you directly."

That surprised Matt. Everyone said no one could see your Talent, but this was the Emperor. The very man who controlled the system. He wouldn't have believed it if he hadn't heard it out of the man's mouth. But why else would he be talking to them now and not just viewing her Talent himself?

Melinda nodded. "I don't mind. It would answer some questions I have as well."

"Good, the six of you are... Wait, why are there seven? Who are you?" Looking at Matt, the Emperor clearly didn't expect him.

"He's an ally and a friend. I trust him. And we've all already shared our info," Melinda spoke up for him.

"Ah. Okay. Still..." the Emperor's golden eyes flicked as if he was reading something, "Matthew Alexander. Age fourteen, well almost fifteen. Tier 1 Talent rating of...detrimental? Hmm. Sponsored by... Hmm... Skills... Hmm... Okay, Matt, I have to ask for your story. This is all just a bit too weird."

Matt felt put under a microscope, the glowing eyes of the ruler of thousands of planets seeming to strip away everything that made him unique. He scrambled for how to explain without lying or admitting he stole something.

"I was given a detrimental Talent at Tier 1, Your Majesty." Matt brought his pad out and flicked his information to the screen. Talent and skill now showing to the seven in the room and the Emperor planets away.

The Emperor read the information over, and Matt continued, "I wasn't able to join the guild with the rating and worked at an inn called Benny's where I met my sponsors and got my skill shard."

The Emperor read the skill information, "Did your sponsors..." He looked away and asked, "Dena and Eric give it to you?"

Matt really wanted to lie and say they did, but he didn't want them to get in trouble. He also figured lying to a Tier 50 would be a recipe for disaster.

Reluctantly, he told the story. Instead of being angry at the theft, the Emperor just chuckled throughout the story.

"Hold on. You said it was called Benny's Inn? Let me pull up the security footage."

A moment later, the screen showed that night. The group of idiots swaggered in at twice the normal speed and replayed the event as Matt described. When the man threw the skill shard, the Emperor's laughter boomed so loudly Matt thought he might hurt himself.

As the footage showed Matt pulling Zephyr out of the brawl, the Emperor asked, "Wait, when did you get the skill shard?"

Matt told him, and the Emperor went back and replayed the moment. "Good hands, kid. From this angle, I can hardly even see it from this footage despite you pointing the moment out."

The video continued to the man waving the mana wand at patrons and demanding Benny let him search others. When they walked out of the frame, it switched to Matt pulling the pad apart and hiding the skill shard, being scanned, and then the man leaving in a huff.

Matt stared at the screen in confusion. There weren't cameras in those locations. He *knew* that for certain. Yet, somehow, the Emperor had video. Unsure of what to make of that, he just moved on.

The man was Tier 50. Matt had no idea what was possible at that level of power.

"So, Your Majesty, that's why Dena and Eric sponsored me."

"While this was very impressive... No, it wasn't. Those two submitted the paperwork for your sponsorship two weeks before this happened and had been there for months."

The Emperor flicked a finger and, on the screen, a sponsorship form to the PlayPen appeared, dated just as the Emperor said. Two full weeks before the duel and theft.

Matt didn't know what to think of that. Dena and Eric had planned on sponsoring him before the spar? He'd thought it was a spur-of-the-moment decision.

"Thanks for the laughs, kid. That was amusing. With your Talent and their recommendation, I expect

great things from you in the next few centuries. You've got guts, and that will take you far if they don't get you killed first. Don't worry about the skill. That fool threw it to attack someone, so that makes it a ranged weapon. Therefore, you just picked up battlefield salvage."

He winked at Matt, then turned back at Melinda. "Now, to you, Melinda. If you would?"

Melinda took her pad and flicked information to the screen.

> **Melinda:**
> - **Talent - Tier 1:** All healing skills are 50% more effective and cost 50% less mana to cast.
> - **Talent - Tier 3:** All healing has the 'Overhealth' effect.
> - **Skills:** [Ranged Heal]

The Emperor's face melted into shock as Matt simply felt confused. With wide eyes, he let out a whistle. The sound created the same effect as before, the world sharpening for an instant.

"Do you mind if I call my chief healer over? Honestly, I want to be fully certain what this means. I have some ideas, but...well, I'd rather get an expert's opinion."

At Melinda's shy nod, he flicked his glowing eyes. Not a full second later, an older man appeared.

After being quickly filled in by the Emperor, he glanced at the screen, "Ah. Well, this is rare. Overhealth has only been seen on some cracked or upgraded skills before. Hmm... To start, Overhealth functions like an

automatic directed healing skill. So, limbs regenerate with no additional effort, and the skill won't stop when a normal undirected skill would reach its limit.

"The [Regeneration] controversy would be a good comparison. It will take some testing to determine if her Talent works the same way. I don't think anyone's ever gotten a Talent with Overhealth before. Not in the Empire, at least."

That seemed to clue the Emperor in, but Matt was still in the dark. Judging by the looks around him, the rest of the party felt the same way.

Looking through the screen, the older man asked, "I'm assuming none of you have heard of that controversy? It usually doesn't matter till well after Tier 15."

Melinda shook her head, so he continued, "Well, there are exceptionally rare upgrade orbs from Tier 14 and above rifts that can upgrade skills within certain limitations. When used, they make significant changes to the skill, and it's always more powerful.

"Well, almost always. There are niche exceptions, which is where [Regeneration] comes in. The skill works like any normal healing skill, you put in mana, and you heal. With the upgrade orb, that changes.

"Then it's more like a channeled skill where you can dump as much mana in at a time as you want to increase the effect. Not only that, but it also changes *how* it heals. If you are a physical cultivator, [Regeneration] is always useful, but it can take months to grow back an arm. With [Upgraded Regeneration], it's like healing a percentage of health. For the same mana cost, it heals better the more physical cultivation you have.

"It's easy to think of with numbers. If you have 100 health, then healing 10 per minute is a lot. But if you have 10,000 health, that same 10 per minute doesn't amount to much. The upgraded [Regeneration] is like healing 1% of your max health a minute. The upgrade is good for physical cultivators who have more health. The non-upgraded is better for mana cultivators who have more mana instead. Some people believe this means we all have hidden health bars and are in a video game, but *they are idiots.*"

Just saying that last part seemed to irritate the older man, and he scoffed. "Physical cultivation makes you stronger and tougher. Of course, it's harder to heal what's harder to damage.

"The true value of Overhealth is seen when someone takes what should be a lethal hit while the upgraded [Regeneration] is active. They can come back from what should have stopped a normal healing spell because they were dead. The Overhealth won't stop when they are considered 'dead' by a normal skill. It only stops when the mana put into the skill has run its course.

"A good example is of a healer with a [Cracked Healing Touch] with an Overhealth effect. Someone's head got smashed flat." The man clapped, "The brain was completely destroyed and, even with the best medical technology and healing, he should have stayed dead. Even if he had been saved, his memories should have been wiped. New gray matter had to grow, after all, to heal him.

"With Overhealth, though, it was like a balloon inflating. Poof, he was up and perfectly fine, memories intact. Closest thing to a miracle you'll ever see."

Melinda's eyes widened. "What does that mean for my Talent?"

The healer exchanged a look with the Emperor, "It means you just became the most valuable healer in the Empire. Every spell you cast will guarantee your party doesn't stay dead. Further testing needs to be done, but I doubt you'll ever need to learn directed healing skills. You'll have an exceptionally lucrative career in medicine, either as a civilian, a delver, or a member of the army. I'd be happy to—"

The Emperor lifted a hand, and the man stopped immediately. "Moon, she and her party are on The Path. We won't interfere."

"Of course, Your Majesty. I got ahead of myself."

The Emperor waved him down and stared through the screen. "If you wish to leave The Path, I won't stop you. I'm sure Harvest will be waiting to snatch you up in a heartbeat. But, instead, I'll just leave the offer on the table if you guys decide to stop climbing or fall off.

"My time on The Path was some of the best of my life. It's where I made the truest of friends and had the moments I'm proudest of. I only made it to Tier 20 before falling off, but those Tiers are truly mine. No one can say I didn't earn those."

The Emperor sighed. "Ascend as much as you can. I can guarantee no one will talk about your Talent, but I want a promise from all of you."

The seven of them nodded. For the first time, the Emperor looked stern. Even the soft light radiating from his eyes grew hard. For a moment, the colors contrasted, and the world sharpened.

It lasted only a breath, but it brought all their focus to the man in front of them. "Don't die. Don't push yourselves to take stupid risks. I don't just say this because of your Talent but because it's a trap. So many try to be

the next Duke Waters and end up as corpses. I've lost too many friends to rifts, and I'll never truly know how they died. Don't add to their numbers."

The Emperor turned to the side. "I've taken up enough of your time. Can you send the other three in? I need to make a few things clear to them. Enjoy your evening and have the party you deserve for reaching Tier 3."

With a smile and a nod, he dismissed them. Hurrying out the door, they found Griff and the other two pacing the hall. When Melinda informed them that the Emperor wanted to see them, the trio looked like they were walking to their executions.

Matt noticed none of them hesitated to enter the room despite their trepidation.

They all looked at each other before Vinnie spoke up, "I need a fucking drink. And a change of underwear."

Chapter 7

Matt woke up fuzzy and lightheaded. After struggling to open his eyes, he found his back pressed against a door.

As the memories came back, he couldn't help but groan. After talking to the Emperor, the seven of them had done as suggested; they had partied.

Hard.

One too many drinks in, Melinda had tried to drag off the older Mathew to consummate their relationship. Preventing that took the other five jointly keeping them away from each other before herding them to their own rooms.

Not five minutes after Melinda had been put into her room, she had tried to sneak into Mathew's. That had left the boys sleeping in Mathew's room to stop him from doing the same.

Matt peered around and saw everyone else was still unconscious. Checking the time, he decided to get breakfast for everyone.

Returning from the dining hall, Matt found Sam with eyes covered, splayed out on the couch. She peeked at him and made 'give me' hands toward the bags of food.

Matt set the bags on the table, "Wake the girls, please." Only a hiss was given in reply.

After waking the boys up, Matt set the table and started eating, slowly. As he picked at the food, the others trickled out of the rooms and to the table.

Mathew was the first to speak. The older boy had the beginnings of a bruise on his cheek. "Who punched me last night? I don't remember."

Matt smirked. "No one. You fell. And your face met a wall. So, if you fought anyone, it was a loss against a wall."

Melinda pointed a finger at Mathew, and a green light danced to him before sinking in, quickly healing the bruise.

The healer repeated the move at all of them. As Matt felt the spell hit him, it washed away his hangover. That spell would have been useful *before* he braved his way to get breakfast for everyone. The dining hall had been painfully noisy.

After eating, they sat around the screen, not having to do anything for a few hours more.

Wanting a break from the news coverage about the Junipers, they found a channel reviewing tournament videos.

"Light and Shadow are still crushing it in the Tier 23 to 24 groups despite being only Tier 21. Truly, it's remarkable to watch the people with the best chance to complete The Path of Ascension. If they do, it will be a first since Duke Waters himself four hundred years ago."

That got Matt's attention. Someone was close to completing The Path? That was huge news. Sadly, they had joined the program at the end. It closed out, and new anchors replaced the last to start a new segment.

Matt turned. "Do you know who they were talking about? Light and Shadow?"

Mathew and Sam covered their faces as Melinda, Kyle, Vinnie, and Tara all jabbered over each other.

"Yeah! How do you not?"

"They are only the best couple ever!"

"Shadow is amazing! She's the best!"

Melinda offered actual useful information, "Light and Shadow are a couple on The Path of Ascension. Just the two of them. They are Tier 21 and only one-hundred-seven years old. At that Tier, they have until one-thirty-eight before they fall off."

Kyle interjected, "They won't fall off. Duke Waters himself met with them and said he'd bet his duchy they are the next to complete The Path. He's never spoken up for a person on The Path before. He can't be wrong."

Tara flicked a picture to the screen. "They are *super* strong. Shadow has some kind of shadow teleporting Talent. Most speculate it's her Tier 3 but, obviously, no one knows for sure. But she's nearly untouchable ever since she also got ahold of [Shadow Manipulation] at some point."

She looked dreamy. "How can you hit someone who disappears at will? Here is their Tier 15 Path of Ascension tournament. It's the last sponsored tournament on The Path. After that, they compete in normal tournaments, usually against a few Tiers higher. Watch this."

On the screen, two party's line-ups were displayed. On the left was a team of five listed with their names and positions. They had a classic composition of tank, melee damage, ranged damage, mage, and healer.

The other side showed just two masked faces, one in the lightest of gray and the other the darkest gray without being black. The names Light and Shadow were under their portraits.

The fight started quickly as Tara jumped ahead of the commentary. The larger party stood across a huge ring that must have spanned a mile across. They quickly turtled up. It did them no good.

Shadow melted into the ground before Light shot forward. The large man crossed the mile in a breath. Light's weapon of choice was a hammer with a head at least five inches across. The way the Tier 15 handled it showed the massive weight of the hammer.

The opposing tank intercepted the blow with his physical shield and a larger copy made by some skill. Upon impact, a blinding light whited out the screen before the camera adjusted for the brightness. When the picture came back, the fight was already over.

A replay showed the events from during the bright flash. The moment Light struck the shield, Shadow rose from the man's own shadow and tore through the rest of the team. Every throat was slit with such speed that, even slowed down, Matt couldn't actually see the blade appear from the darkness, only follow the clutching of throats.

The tank didn't fare any better. From that one blow, his shield was mangled, and his heavy plate armor was dented to such a degree Matt was sure his chest was crushed.

Matt couldn't believe it and had to ask, "That wasn't an exhibition match? That other party was on The Path? No way they were defeated in a single attack."

Vinnie answered with a huge grin, "Yup, and a solid party as well. They were Tier 15s who delved rifts at Tier 16. There just isn't anything to do against massive power differences."

"Why didn't they just counter the flash Light used? Then Shadow couldn't have gotten to their entire team. Seems like an easy way to counter the duo. Light seems more like a support that enables Shadow than someone powerful on his own." Matt still couldn't believe what he had just watched.

Tara scoffed. "Yeah, people had the same thought before. Not hard to think of after all. It doesn't matter, though. Light could have handled that entire team himself. Look, this was a 1 vs 1 back when Light was Tier 10."

With a flick of her finger, a new video started. This time, two announcers talked before the pre-match introductions.

"Pepper, do you think Light has a chance here? His opponent is a peak Tier 10, and Light only broke through the Tier 10 wall two days ago."

"I don't think he has a chance. We've seen how he makes Shadow stronger and gives her mobility, but he hasn't done much himself this entire tournament in the party vs party brackets. Now that it's down to the 1 vs 1 duels, I think it's the end for this half of the winning party."

"Agreed. I think he's out of the tournament this match. His opponent is a hybrid tank with [Projected Bulwark] as his main skill. It's going to be hard to break through that. In the team fights, it was Shadow who took him out. Even damage heavy Pathers will have a hard time getting through that. I just don't think he has the power to do it."

The countdown ended, and the man in full plate looked at Light. The moment the counter hit zero, he pushed out his shield, and a ten-foot-tall replica made from mana appeared from it. The man taunted, "Let's see you get through this without your little whore in the shadows."

Light pulled a longsword from seemingly nowhere, Matt assumed it was a spatial device, and slashed in a lazy X pattern. From the blade, two crescents of energy shot out, racing toward the armored man. Then Light thrust the sword out, and a third beam appeared.

The first two [Mana Slash]s cracked the large projection before the third energy attack pierced through the [Projected Bulwark] and the man behind it.

The announcers went wild, "He doesn't have [Mana Thrust]. I checked. Was that a thrust with [Mana Slash]? That's impossible! The skill needs a slashing movement to discharge the stored energy. This is completely unheard of—"

"Effin—"

Tara paused the recording. "See? They! Are! Monsters! That was them at Tier 15, and then Light at Tier 10. Now, they don't even have to try to win against Tier 23s. And they are so young, they aren't even rushing the last few Tiers like Duke Waters had to."

Melinda chimed in as she slumped back into her chair. "They are so strong. I wish I could have half of their power someday."

Matt was aghast. That was how top Tier cultivators fought? Matt thought over the [Mana Slash] that had been used as a thrust. He wanted a small part of that power. That was where the peak was.

He wondered about the masks, so he asked the group. Vinnie responded the fastest, "It's not super common, but it isn't rare either. Not everyone wants the notoriety of climbing The Path. So, the masks."

"So, no one knows what they look like?"

Tara answered him, "Nope, not even a little. Duke Waters killed like twenty people when they revealed his face during his climb. He was staying anonymous, but someone snuck a camera into a private changing room. Then he couldn't go anywhere without crowds blocking his way or dealing with assassins from the other Great Powers. He's made it very clear, anyone who breaks the rule will regret it."

Melinda added, "It only happened once since, and he kept his word. A team at Tier 7 got outed, and he slaughtered the entire company responsible."

"That's not true. He only killed those who ordered it and did it. He only killed like...three people. That bullshit about him slaughtering everyone is propaganda against him," Vinnie countered Melinda's statement.

Matt tuned out the bickering.

He wanted that power. How would it feel to smash everyone, even Tiers above your own? His resolve to delve and climb The Path of Ascension grew every time he pictured that sword thrust.

Matt had just entered the rift and could tell something was wrong. It was in the air, in his spirit...in his gut.

In the first room, he found proof. Where one unclothed and shoddily armed goblin should be, he found three goblins clad in the scale armor usually only found in the final room of the rift.

Matt had been planning on using a shield and mace for this delve but quickly stowed them in the sack and drew his longsword.

No reason to risk something new without my best weapon.

Matt debated leaving to report the anomaly, but then he would lose out on his chance to delve. And it wasn't like these goblins could hurt him with his [Cracked Phantom Armor] active.

What do I have to fear?

At worst, there would be three hobgoblins, and then he could retreat to the entrance.

Matt advanced. It took more time but, through every room, he found three times the usual number of goblins.

Halfway through, he had developed an inkling of what might be going on. He'd heard about something that rifts would do on rare occasions: a rift challenge. If Matt remembered correctly, it could happen to any Tier of rift but was incredibly rare.

The topic had been covered in his introduction information, but he couldn't remember most of the details. The statistic of one in a million tickled his memory though.

Matt did know one thing, the greater the relative risk, the better the reward. That mantra was always mentioned when delvers made daring risks and became legends overnight.

The catch was that greater rewards came with greater challenges.

If his vague memories were right, a Tier 1 rift going through a rift challenge put its power around Tier 2 strength. But the rewards would dwarf any normal Tier 2 rift rewards.

That thought pushed Matt on. If a Tier 1 rift couldn't even scratch him, then he could handle a Tier 2 rift, so long as he proceeded slowly and carefully.

Would Light and Shadow have run from this? No. They're so strong, they would wrap this up without breaking a sweat. This is my chance. I could get Tier 2 mana stones. If I'm lucky, I could even get a Tier 2 essence stone, or maybe something better! I can buy anything I want with that kind of wealth.

Matt knew greed was driving him forward but couldn't stop. Risk paired with reward was the one constant of delving rifts.

In the second-to-last room, the enemies changed from fully armored goblins to the normal hobgoblins.

The sight almost made him turn around, but he still hesitated.

If the boss was just a training monster before, what's waiting for me in the final room?

Matt decided to at least peek at what was waiting for him.

Even if I turn around now, I've still gotten more essence from this than in three normal delves, and way more gear to sell. This is profitable either way. But I should at least check the final room.

Matt finished off the three hobgoblins with little difficulty. He had been fighting them for almost four months now and could predict every one of their moves.

Peering into the final room, Matt froze. Instead of the normal five goblins and one hobgoblin, it was five hobgoblins and what Matt could only identify as an orc. The large, tusked monster was at least 6'5" and had a build so wide it looked stocky even at that height. It wasn't fat, though. The muscles rippling under its armor spoke of the monster's strength.

Matt glanced from the pile of armor and weapons he had dragged here and back to the orc. Then he looked to the reward distortion.

It shone with whitish-blue light to his spiritual sense. The glow spoke to Matt, whispering of power and fame.

In his mind, he could see Light and Shadow fighting. A single blow of Light's weapon crushing a tank at his own Tier, who was also on The Path at Tier 15. He envisioned crushing someone most people thought of as the best of the best in a single blow.

The Emperor's words from weeks prior rang in his mind, "In a few hundred years, I expect great things from you."

Heading back felt cowardly. Matt wanted greatness. He wanted the power, the fame.

He stared at the reward distortion. He wanted that item. He craved it.

Matt stepped into the room.

When he stepped through the entrance, the situation immediately grew worse. The hobs, who he now saw were in much better armor than usual, charged at him directly. The orc leader pulled a throwing ax off his belt and hurled it at him just inside the entrance.

Matt sidestepped it, but the wind of its passage and the spray of chipped stones from the wall stressed [Cracked

Phantom Armor] in a way that the boss hobgoblins never had.

This may have been a bad idea.

There was no more time for regret. The hobs were on him, and he was forced to retreat to the left. He managed to bait out and punish an attack by the closest hob, drawing his sword under its helmet to slit its throat.

He sidestepped to keep the orc from throwing another ax at him while he was open but, as the hobgoblin blocked his view, Matt noticed a smirk on the orc's tusked face.

He threw himself to the side. As he came up from the roll, he saw the hob in front of him take the projectile to the back. The ax head was buried through the armor, down to the shaft. The power of the projectile sent the hob flying into its two remaining kin. Matt took the chance to finish the downed opponents with quick thrusts of his blade before they could stand.

The struck monster was a grim indication of what *he* would look like if a throwing ax ever landed.

As he stabbed down for the final time, Matt heard the telltale *whoosh* of an attack and rolled again. The throwing ax crashed off the wall. He looked to the orc as it lifted a shield and spear, charging at him.

Quickly retrieving his dropped longsword in an awkward scramble, Matt deflected a probing thrust, only to narrowly avoid taking a shield bash when he stepped to the orc's left.

He looked to the entrance to escape. This wasn't a fight he could win, but the orc had curled around his path and blocked his retreat.

The pull of the rewards and promises of glory were gone. Only terror remained as he realized what fate awaited him if he made a single mistake from here on.

Matt flicked a strike at the orc's legs as it pulled its spear back from another light jab at his torso. The orc just stepped back and thrust again with the spear, shield raised and at the ready, not worrying about the light blow.

This orc is keeping me back with his height and weapon length advantage. What should I do? What can I do?

Matt deflected the spear again, but instead of using the flat of his blade, he used the edge in a heavy chop. He'd be spending money to have the blade fixed from striking the hardwood, but it was better than dying.

As the orc repeatedly attacked with the haft of the spear, Matt retreated in circles, parrying each blow. When he felt enough damage was done, he dodged to the left and chopped the head off the spear, striking the weakened shaft where his repeated attacks chipped at the wood.

He went to press his advantage, but the orc reacted quickly for the first time. It discarded the now shortened shaft, covering itself with the shield while reaching for something behind its back.

Matt drew his dagger with his left hand and threw it at the orc's face. The dagger was going to miss, but the orc instinctively raised his shield to block the thrown weapon, and Matt took the opportunity to thrust with his sword.

He caught the orc in the guts, and when the weapon was deep inside monster flesh, he pulled his blade to the left with all his might to try and eviscerate the monster. However, the orc was faster than Matt predicted. The boss slammed its shield into his still embedded longsword and ripped the weapon out of Matt's hands, along with its guts, and stepped over the clattering sword.

That's when Matt noticed a red haze appearing around the orc. He knew what the skill was and immediately retreated, leaving his sword on the ground. He was entirely unwilling to stay anywhere near the monster.

The skill was [Berserker's Rage]. It was rarely used by humans due to its reliance on taking injuries to fuel stronger attacks and increased speeds.

The skill had a nasty side effect. Any wounds were much harder to heal when active, so only the truly desperate used it. And monsters. Matt had heard it was fairly common to see when fighting melee monsters. He just hadn't expected a Tier 1 rift, even one under the influence of a rift challenge, to produce a Tier 3 monster.

Matt turned and ran to where a thrown ax had bounced off the wall.

He heard a whooshing sound from behind and tried to dodge but was hit by the thrown shield in the left side and arm. Bones shattered in a flare of pain, his arm and several ribs breaking under the hit. [Cracked Phantom Armor] flickered as he focused on rebuilding the skill structure in his spirit after the massive blow.

The impact sent him sprawling, and his skill deactivated long enough for him to scrape his face and good hand along the stone floor. Quickly, he forced himself to stand through the pain. The only good thing was that he had landed on the ax, and as he stood, he swung it where he expected the boss monster.

The orc was faster.

Under the suicidal influence of [Berserker's Rage], it had charged with arms spread, intent to take his smaller human form down, and use its weight and strength advantages in a grapple.

Matt's wild swing had cut into the outstretched hand, but the pain meant nothing to the monster. Unable to get completely out of the way, he was bowled over. Only [Cracked Phantom Armor] reduced the impact enough to prevent it from overwhelming his senses.

Scrambling to his feet one handed, he turned and ran before the orc could finish gathering itself for another charge.

If that brute gets a good grip on me, I'm done for. I'll never break free before he crushes me, [Cracked Phantom Armor] or no.

The orc had already proven even a glancing attack was strong enough to overwhelm the skill.

Matt reached the center of the room and turned, ax raised, to see the charging orc just feet away. The monster's stance was low, with arms over its head, primed to protect itself from the raised ax.

I don't want to die here.

I can't lose in a Tier 1 rift.

Matt firmed his will. Panicking wouldn't do him any good, he needed to take full advantage of his one edge. The orc was using [Berserker's Rage], and that made it less rational. That was his only chance.

The monster approached with bounding strides, it was so fast, Matt only had a moment to make a decision.

I will be endless. This cannot be my end!

Matt had an instant of clarity. The world sharpened, and the pain of his broken arm faded.

His overhead blow wouldn't work, so he dropped the ax and abandoned that plan. With his right hand, he picked up the broken haft of the spear, wedging its iron-clad butt into the stony ground and bracing it with a foot.

The enraged orc ran onto the length of wood, impaling itself on the broken remains of its own weapon.

Dying hands tried to get a grip on Matt as they went tumbling, but [Cracked Phantom Armor] provided enough defense to outlast the orc's final, desperate struggles.

A massive amount of essence entered his spirit. It felt like he had eaten far too much, but instead of his stomach being bloated, it was his spirit. Some essence was lost, but he couldn't find it in himself to care.

On his back, Matt gazed past the ceiling before starting to laugh. The blood he tasted didn't diminish his joy in the slightest, it was simply proof he was the victor.

That had been exhilarating. He felt *truly* alive for the first time. He had fought a monster that was probably at Tier 3, and he had won.

Still lying on the cool stone of the floor, Matt looked to the orc a few feet away. He was pretty sure only monsters at the very peak of Tier 2 or Tier 3 had skills, but it hadn't come up in his reviews yet.

Matt laughed again, but the pain in his left side stopped him from doing so for long.

Looking down, he saw nothing but the blue of his skill armor, but he felt the wetness clinging to his clothes inside [Cracked Phantom Armor].

Huh? [Cracked Phantom Armor] keeps my blood inside? Why?

Carefully, he stood up and fetched the ax he had baited the orc with. He was taking a trophy. With careful maneuvering, Matt decapitated the orc and proceeded to gather the armor from where he had stashed it and all the metal from the final room.

His sack was nearly too heavy to lift with his injuries. Only with great care and patience was Matt able to get everything to the tear in space that was the exit.

He was growing foggier as his adrenaline faded, and each movement became stiffer.

Matt was damned if he was going to leave a single thing behind. Even if he got Melinda to heal him, healing was always expensive, and he refused to take advantage of his friends. He had seen best friends turn to enemies at the orphanage over items worth far less than a healer's skill.

Gingerly, after he moved the pile of loot to the exit rift, he looked to the final reward distortion. Now that the fight was over, it once again called to him with blueish light.

He paused. Some instinct told him this was a pivotal moment.

The pain in his side grew as the adrenaline completely faded, and Matt stood frozen in place.

He knew there was no proof that a reward wasn't already set when the rift was created, but this felt like a time to lean into superstition. On instinct more than thought, Matt sent out a pulse of essence. Nothing had changed, but he felt that was the moment.

In the place of the small distortion was a... Matt wasn't sure what it was. It looked like a fist-sized egg made of ice.

He knew bondable creatures were possible rift rewards, but he had only seen one in a movie. Beyond that, he had only heard of them as voluntary contracts with wild beasts, o. he vaguely thought there was something about buying one, but he was too lightheaded to dredge up the memory.

Matt hated that so much information was kept from the low Tiered cultivators. He sighed, nothing he could do about it now except get it scanned and evaluated.

Looking at the orc's head at the top of the sack made Matt smile again.

The risk was sky high, and my reward should match that.

Matt pulled out his pad and typed a message to Melinda asking for her help. The message would be sent once he left the rift, and he could deal with broken bones for the time it took to get to the living quarters on the edge of the island.

He wasn't looking forward to the ride back from the center of the island, but if he was going to pay a healer's outrageous fees, he wanted the money to go to a friend instead of a stranger.

Broken bones weren't life-threatening, they just hurt. But Matt was old friends with pain.

After he placed the large egg next to the orc head, he lifted the sack, hissing as the weight put pressure on his broken ribs. Stepping through the portal, he was quickly seen and helped by the waiting guards. As he was led out of the room, he tried to decline the offers of a healer, saying he had one on the way.

Before Matt could make his way to the check-out desk, he heard Melinda.

How is she here so fast?

He couldn't understand what was happening with the ever-growing darkness encroaching on his vision. He had taken much longer than usual to finish the rift. It should have been well after they usually finished their own delve. Even after becoming Tier 3s, they never took more than three hours to finish clearing a rift.

He was grabbed by Melinda and, as her hand touched him, he felt her [Ranged Heal] soothing the pain slightly.

When her face moved in front of his, he still couldn't understand. Her mouth was moving, but no sound was coming out.

"Deactivate your skill. It's interfering with my healing."

Matt felt the fog lift in his mind enough for the words to sink in and stopped feeding mana to [Cracked Phantom Armor]. As he did, he felt wetness moving down his side.

As the pressure from his skill ended and the broken bones shifted again, hands guided him to the ground. He tried to protest but was overruled and manhandled down.

More gentle, soothing energy washed the aches and pains away, and he finally becoming more clear-headed. Melinda's Talent healed the injuries as if they never happened.

"You back with us, Matt? What happened?"

Melinda kneeled over him, and an older lady in healer's robes stood behind her.

"Yeah, I'm good. Think I had a concussion."

"No shit! And your left side was all fucked up. You realize you had a two-inch chunk cut out of your side?"

It had felt far worse than that, but Matt kept that to himself. "I think it was a rift challenge. It was way harder than it should have been."

The older healer standing over them interjected, "That's a bold claim, young man. Do you have any proof? Or are you trying to save face because you fucked up?"

That irritated Matt. Who was she to judge him? She implied he couldn't handle a Tier 1 rift.

"Look in the sack and tell me what you think. It should be all the proof I need."

Matt got the shock he expected, but not for the reason he thought. Instead of pulling the orc head out, the healer removed the large egg made of ice.

"I'll give you a million credits for this," she said and tucked the egg away.

Matt shouted, "Fuck no!" as he struggled up. Melinda kept a firm grip on him, preventing his movement.

The healer hesitated but looked at the guards before saying, "Ten million."

Matt struggled to his feet. "Give it back!"

Who did this woman think she was?

The commotion had drawn the guard captain to see what was wrong. As he took in the scene, he said, "Iris, you know that pressuring a sponsored individual is against policy and trying to lowball a prize is even more of a crime."

"It's not like he would make good use of it. The idiot almost got killed in a Tier 1 rift. He should take some money and go live a normal life." The healer holding his reward took a step away after saying that.

The guard captain walked over to the sack and pulled the orc head out. "Sure looks like to me and my spiritual sense that this, 'idiot who almost got himself killed in a Tier 1 rift,' killed a Tier 3 orc using [Berserker's Rage] before it died. If what I'm feeling is right. Am I lying as well, Iris?"

Matt was startled. How could the guard tell all of that? Was his spiritual sense that good? Or was it something else? Maybe some hidden aspect of the monster he couldn't recognize.

That represented the power he wanted. If he had power like that, this arrogant healer would never dare to try and steal what was his.

The guard captain continued, "You know as well as I do that a Tier 3 can only appear in a Tier 1 with a rift challenge. And you want to try and steal from someone on The Path? Someone on The Path who can kill a Tier 3 at Tier 1? If the Empire didn't hunt you down, how long do you think you'd last before he did?" As he finished, Griff suddenly appeared. "And I already reported this incident." The captain shrugged as if it was already settled.

The healer looked pale but still tried to defend herself with Matt's egg clutched to her chest. "This is wasted on him. Ten million is more than fair. I—"

Griff interrupted her, "Iris, you know stealing from someone who is on The Path while working at a PlayPen is a capital offense?" Iris tried to speak, but Griff cut her off. "And ten million for that egg is stealing. Iris, you know it, and so does everyone here. Now, how about you put—"

"It should be mine! I've been healing these brats for so long! I *deserve* this. If I can't have it, he sure ca—"

Matt's heart stopped as Iris moved to smash the egg, but before she could do more than raise her hand, Griff had already moved. He held her raised hand with his right, and his entire left arm was through her chest.

With a shake, he took hold of Matt's egg and dislodged the dead healer. "Captain, I'm sure you and your men will act as witnesses for the investigation. The cameras should have gotten everything, but we'll still need to go through the motions."

With one arm covered in blood, Griff looked at the woman on the floor. "Why? Why do you all insist on making my life difficult?"

He handed the egg to Matt and peeked at the orc head with a nod.

"Well, the events shouldn't be that hard to explain. Matt, I'm assuming you found yourself in a rift challenge and decided *not* to leave?"

Matt, now having been completely healed and only sore, nodded.

"I remembered they were rare an—"

Griff sighed and cut him off with closed eyes. "They aren't actually that rare. Solo delvers find them more often, one in say ten to twenty thousand delves. It's the rifts way to get a free kill. They get stronger from every death inside them."

That was common knowledge. Rifts could grow slowly over time, but deaths accelerated the process.

"Rifts aren't alive, but they do run like magical code, with a lot of 'if-then' statements. If the group that enters is stronger than it, then the rift uses as little essence as it can to not waste resources. If the group is weaker than it, then it will send the normal monster. Because why waste the essence?"

The large man shook his hand, trying to get the blood off it. "But there is a gray spot between the two. If the rift's calculations lead it to believe it can get a kill from boosting its power a bit, *and* it thinks it won't spend more on a rift challenge than it would get for killing the delvers, a challenge will appear. The odds go up if the rift is low on essence."

Seeing the blood refusing to come off, the man summoned a towel from nowhere and wiped off the blood. "Most solo delvers are smart enough to just back out and re-enter. It's essence expensive, and the rift can't recycle the monsters. Rift challenges have a survival

rate of about one in a million for solo delvers. It's better for those on The Path because most are stronger than average, but it's still near one in five hundred thousand. The rifts only do it when the math adds up in their favor. So, *please* explain why you were stupid enough to *actually* attempt it."

Matt suddenly felt very foolish. The information Griff stated cleared up the confusion he had and jogged his memory of his brief when he first arrived on the island. He had thought there was a one in a million chance to get a rift challenge, not one in a million chance to *survive* one.

"I, uhh...misremembered it as being one in a million to find one and...didn't want to pass the chance up." He swallowed hard at the look in the man's eyes.

Griff ground the heels of his hands into his eyes, not noticing or caring about the blood covering his left hand. Then he wordlessly screamed into his hands.

Matt suddenly felt *really* scared. Would Griff hurt him if he snapped?

After he stopped screaming, Griff took his hands off his face. "I can't even accurately prove to you how dangerous that was. I just hope you remember that in the future the difference between Tiers is larger. Tier 1 to 3 is manageable. As you advance, the gulf just increases."

The bloody handprint covering half his face gave each word a menacing aura.

"It's not manageable by everyone, or even most people, but it's not completely unheard of. As you ascend to higher Tiers, it takes more essence to advance, and that makes the gaps between them wider. There's a reason those who complete The Path are so rare. It's a race where you have to fight three or more Tiers above yourself, and at Tier 20 or higher, it's nearly impossible to cross Tiers. That's why those who can are so highly valued."

Griff was working himself up, and even the guard captain had retreated. Matt felt frozen and vulnerable with just Melinda and company directly behind him.

"There has been one person, *one single fucking person*, to do it in the last thousand years. One thousand fucking years. Can you imagine how many people have been born in the Empire in the last millennium?"

Matt didn't think he was supposed to answer that, but when Griff paused, he opened his mouth before Griff's eyes refocused. "I just looked it up. About 714 billion per year. Give or take some. Seven. Hundred. And fourteen. *Billion* people per year, over the last millennium. Not a single one has managed to replicate Duke Waters feat."

The man looked pleading as he said, "Matt, you are not better than the *seven hundred and fourteen trillion* people before you."

Griff took a deep breath and sighed. He looked like he'd aged ten years.

"And the worst thing is, you got rewarded for your reckless behavior. Tens of millions will die trying to get the same reward as you did. If you care at all, you'll keep the source of that—" he waved at the egg in Matt's hand, "a secret.

"Just say you got lucky in the normal rift. Or better yet, don't answer at all. Because if it gets out that it was from a rift challenge, every new person on any PlayPen for the next decade will try it instead of escaping as is recommended. They will attempt to repeat your feat, and *so* few of them will make it out alive. Even fewer will make it through alive and victorious as you did."

Matt felt terrible. He hadn't thought his actions out that far. What was this egg? Was it so valuable to send people to their deaths to risk getting something similar?

The icy egg suddenly felt heavier than the orc corpse had when it tried to end his life with its own.

"Melinda, is he okay to move?"

The healer just nodded at Griff's question, not daring to speak.

"You can all go home. I beg you not to talk about this. I really do. I just had to kill a Tier 8 Healer because of it. Please, don't get more people killed. I am *sick* of watching children die."

With that, Griff was gone.

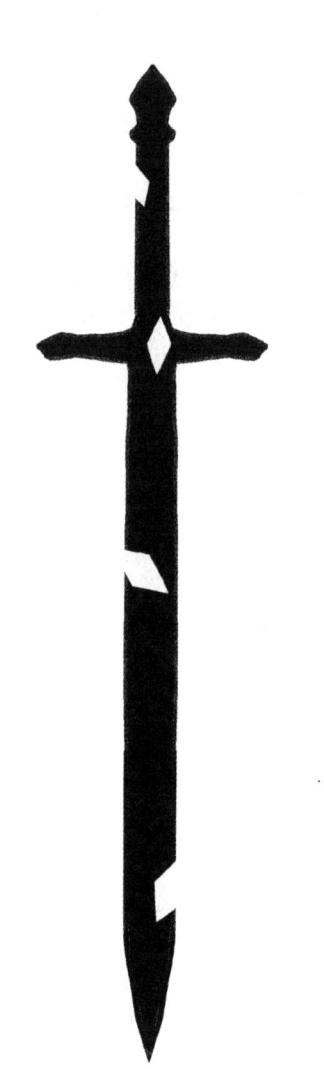

Chapter 8

Usually, Matt rode the bus that made trips between the rift and developed area of the island, but not tonight. None of them wanted to wait near the rifts and left quickly after.

He looked down at the trophy he had been so proud of and felt sick. With an effort that surprisingly didn't strain his recently healed body, he threw the orc's head into the woods.

It had transformed from a symbol of his bravery and victory to a token of his stupidity.

He nearly died and had wanted to take the head of his fallen foe and proudly proclaim he had killed it. A statement Matthew Alexander was the next Duke Waters. The next Light and Shadow.

The encounter now tasted like ashes.

Healer Iris's greed toward the cold egg in his hand had angered him, and that still had him simmering. If not for the Empire and its rules, the strong would be able to

take anything they wanted. Matt wasn't strong. He was protected by a Tier 50 who was planets away and wanted people to grow and not be oppressed.

That wasn't *his* strength. The healer should have followed the rules but, instead, tried to crush Matt with her money and power. Griff was a better person than Iris, but what if he hadn't been?

Everything he risked his life for could have been snatched in an instant.

He did not want to... No... He could *never* be weak again. Iris reminded him of how he felt at eight when the rift break had torn everyone he had ever loved away from him. He knew he had only been a child, but if people had been stronger, the rift break would have been easily pushed back. If the Junipers had done their duty, he wouldn't have lost everything he held dear.

Power is the only way to protect what I care about. Is that all that matters?

Matt wanted that power. He looked at Melinda, Mathew, Kyle, Sam, Vinnie, and Tara. He wanted to be able to protect his friends who had run to help, even if he didn't know how they got there so fast. Now wasn't the time to ask, but he made a note to return the favor however he could. They had been friends through the good times and parties but, tonight, they had proven they were there in the bad times as well.

Griff had been right. Matt could admit that. He may have misremembered the information about rift challenges, but he had played it smart and cautious until he had seen the reward distortion. If he hadn't been blinded by his avarice, he could have retreated and still could have made good gains in both essence and credits.

The fight with the orc could have gone worse in a thousand different ways. Any misstep or dodge in the wrong direction, and he could have been killed. He had only been hit with a single thrown shield, and it destroyed the left side of his body, and that was through his armor skill.

Matt knew he was lucky it was only a glancing blow, and that [Cracked Phantom Armor] had stopped him from bleeding out. His left side was covered in blood from only a few moments between the skill turning off and Melinda healing him.

The area felt oddly perfect to his senses. The wounds were healed and not even sore to the touch. Matt looked to the healer. He owed her. He couldn't imagine how to even begin to repay the debt, but he promised himself he would one day.

He would become strong enough that he wouldn't need to rely on the protection of the Empire and the Emperor. He wouldn't need to lean on his friends. He would grow strong enough to be able to support them as they had supported him. To do that, he needed to get better.

As the long walk ended and the residential area was in sight, Melinda broke the long silence. "Healer Iris wasn't a good person. Rumor had it she was here because she tried to extort someone while acting as an official Healer.

It's just a rumor, but she's always been an asshole. Never willing to share techniques or offer suggestions when I'm learning."

Mathew chimed in after his girlfriend, "Well, I think her actions tonight kinda prove those rumors right."

"Yeah, I guess they do." Melinda sounded resigned to the fate of the late healer.

Tara quietly asked, "Did Griff have to kill her? That seems a little excessive with his power."

Kyle quietly answered her, "Yeah, he did. Theft of rift rewards is considered banditry, and the punishment for that is always death. My combat tutor talked about it. He said it's considered kinder to just kill them and avoid the publicity."

"That's stupid. We shouldn't kill anyone that easily. She could have been given a second chance."

"She was on her second chance. No way she deserved a third. She tried to steal from Matt. Are you saying she should?" Kyle snapped back.

"No, I—"

Matt felt the need to interject before they got farther off track, "Thanks for the quick reaction. I swear I'll—"

He was stopped as a red-eyed Melinda jumped in front of him, finger in his face. "If you say 'pay me back,' by every bad thing I can think of, I. Will. Hurt. You. We help each other. That's what friends do. If you had the chance, I'm sure you'd do the same. All that's needed is a thank you."

As he opened his mouth to protest, Melinda glared harder. "Matthew Alexander, the next words that leave your mouth better not be anything other than 'thank you,' Do. Not. Fucking. Test. Me."

Matt acquiesced. "Thank you, Melinda." He looked to the rest of her party. "Thanks to all of you. I just don't want you guys to feel like I'm only friends with you for free heals. I've seen friendships end over far less. And I value our friendship too much."

Mathew looped an arm around his shoulder. "It's not like we haven't had to fend off people who just wanted to cozy up to us for Melinda's abilities. It's easy to tell who's who."

"Also, as the healer who treated you, I'm banning you from delving for the next two shifts," Melinda sounded smug at the proclamation.

"You can do that? What about your...?" He paused, not wanting to say it out loud, "You know what."

"Yeah, and I'll make it three if you give me any more lip. And it's not fully tested. While it should remove the healing cooldown, I don't trust it yet."

Looking at her still red eyes and slight sniffle she was trying to hide, Matt didn't feel it would be smart to call her bluff.

"Okay, but you need to explain what happened," Sam steered the conversation into safer waters.

"After you all explain how you got to the rift so fast."

"Easy. You're usually out of the rift way before us, and when you didn't answer our message, we got worried. We saw your pad hadn't gone online since your rift time, so we waited outside in case you needed Melinda's help. We know your skill makes it so you can't really get hurt in a Tier 1 rift, so we got worried."

Kyle added, "Unless he's crazy enough to fight a Tier 3. I'm surprised you can walk, Matt."

Matt didn't know what he was talking about. Walk? His legs hadn't been injured.

"With the size of those balls on you, I'm surprised you aren't just bouncing down the road on them."

Ohhhhhh.

The attempt at humor didn't quite land, but he appreciated the effort. Tara added, "Yeah, give us the story. How did you do it?"

So, Matt told them. Their reactions made him feel a little better after Griff's dressing down. But he still felt Griff had been mostly right, even if a little harsh. He definitely would make a different decision if presented with the same situation a second time.

The incident felt as if it had happened to someone else once the adrenaline had run its course.

As they got to the housing complex, Matt was urged to scan the egg, and after he had, they rushed to the group's suite to view the results privately.

Bound Pet: Arctic Fox.

Elemental Affinity: Ice.

The group then looked up how to bond the pet, which was like bonding a skill shard. Send essence in, and then a few days later the creature would hatch.

That sparked a debate on why a fox was in an egg until Melinda, who looked up the procedures with Matt, saw an author's note, which she read out loud.

"Guys, holy shit. This explains why Iris tried so hard to steal the egg! Listen to this, '*While arctic foxes aren't particularly stronger or weaker than other bound pets, they are prized for their beauty. Most eggs that are placed on the market go for fifty Tier 11 mana stones.*' Wow, that's a lot of credits."

Then Melinda straightened in realization, "That bitch Iris only offered you ten million credits."

"Wait, why is it worth fifty Tier 11 mana stones and not five Tier 12 mana stones?" Kyle asked.

That led to more searching for the group to learn that after Tier 5, mana stones increased the total mana they held, leading to a ratio jump of fifty to one. Then another jump every ten Tiers until it was a thousand to one at Tier 50.

Strategic resources like shielding and rift disrupters used millions of mana a second at the higher Tiers. There the mana capacity of rift-made mana stones was valued much more, so the price increased faster than the total mana. Manmade mana stones that were rechargeable were only able to hold 200 mana at the same size of the rift-made ones. After that, they ballooned in size.

Matt and the others spent the rest of the evening trying to decide on what to name the unhatched arctic fox, looking at the available pictures with a chorus of oohs and aahs.

They even watched some combat footage with companion arctic foxes. There wasn't much, but what they found impressed him. The lowest Tier of video they found was Tier 7, but the fox had created a small blizzard and shot icicles at the targets.

He thought about selling the egg, but the thought was quickly pushed aside. He had fought too hard to give even an average pet away. The money would be nice in the short term, but a bond would be a partner that could travel the Tiers with him. Added to the fact foxes seemed to be natural mages just solidified his choice.

He could use more ranged attacks in his arsenal.

There was no way he was selling the prize of his rift challenge.

He looked at the egg in his lap, the PlayPenNet said it could take anywhere from one to three days to hatch, but he wanted it to hatch now. Or rather, in the morning. He was tired and needed to get pet supplies.

Shit. What do foxes need? Are they like cats? Dogs? I've never had a pet.

The next morning, Matt stood outside Griff's door. It was early enough that Matt hadn't expected the man to be in, but the light was on, so he knocked.

"Come in."

He did so, and Griff looked surprised to see him.

The Tier 15 gave Matt a tired smile. "Sorry about yesterday. I shouldn't have yelled at you. I had just come back from a party's funeral, but that doesn't excuse how I acted. I shouldn't have lost my temper like that, and I apologize. That was both unprofessional and wrong of me."

Matt was surprised. This wasn't how he expected this to go. He had planned to apologize and thank the older man.

"No, you were right. It was stupid to push on. I got greedy, and it almost got me killed. I thought over the fight a lot last night, and it went about as well as it could have. I'm pretty good, but I know I'm not good enough to guarantee a kill on a Tier 3. I got lucky."

This next part felt embarrassing, but Matt pushed on, "I thought I could be the next Light and Shadow. I told myself to take it easy and not risk it. And I did until the last room. Before that, only the last three rooms could even get through my skill, and they were just the normal hobgoblins. Even three of them weren't so strong that I was concerned at all."

Swallowing, Matt finished, "And I looked in and saw the hobs and the orc. I knew I should have turned around, but when I saw the reward distortion, it felt..." Matt looked down and pulled the large ice egg out of the backpack he was carrying it with.

"It felt like this was my chance to be great. I considered myself too good and skilled to waste the opportunity. I swore I'd be the next person to complete The Path. Looking back, they were just bullshit justifications to be greedy. I looked up what little info I could find, and Light and Shadow were clearing Tier 1 rifts at Tier 1. They weren't great and strong until they got skills and experience. I don't have either. But I thought I did, especially after winning."

His voice broke slightly, so he swallowed and continued, "So...I just wanted to thank you for the reality check. And stopping that healer from stealing my prize."

Griff had leaned back in his chair during Matt's stumbling apology and wore a slight smile after Matt finished.

"Well, I didn't expect that. A lot of people don't appreciate the fact they're not the hero of the story, that they won't get to save the Empire and get the girl. I learned that lesson much later in life. I thought I was hot shit, thought I was the next Duke Waters. I believed

it, too. My whole team thought we were going to be the next greats.

"So, we started delving into Tier 12s at Tier 10. It's how we fell off The Path. My wife was chopped in half, and the other two of my teammates were moments from death but, thankfully, we were all able to retreat with our lives. And the worst part is, I didn't even get a bruise."

The man met Matt's eyes, but he was clearly somewhere else. "That was the day I learned I wasn't special. My wife and two of my best friends were almost the price I had to pay to learn that lesson."

Griff turned a picture on his desk around, him holding a woman smiling up at him with another couple doing the same.

"I treasure them more than advancing fast. The prizes are an illusion, Matt. After Tier 5's free skill shard, The Path is *not* worth risking everything. You know how age works with cultivation?"

Matt shook his head. "I know the higher you get until Tier 15 you live longer, but I don't know the details."

"At Tier 10, you'll have a life expectancy of almost seven hundred years, Matt. Seven hundred years is a long time. Those who go slow and steady are far more likely to hit Tier 15, and those who do hit Tier 15 slowly are more likely to reach Tier 25. People like to fixate on The Path, but it's a charnel house."

"Then why is The Path a thing? It seems wasteful." Matt wasn't just happy to move on from his blunder but was actually interested.

"It is and it isn't. I wish it weren't so, but The Path is a net positive. The Empire isn't the only Tier 50 power out there. There are seven others of relative strength. And all have some variation of The Path. It shows everyone

else that our younger generation is strong. It's an internal competition to show external power that the Great Powers put on.

"The last war the Empire fought was six or seven hundred years ago. It was a tame war as far as those things go, and yet, we still lost eight hundred million people."

"What was the war about?" Matt was curious now.

Griff laughed, but there was no humor in it. "A Tier 30 world was found with natural portals to both Empire territory and the republic. Both sides claimed it, and so blood was shed. Do you know why we haven't had another?"

Matt shook his head, so Griff continued, "Duke Waters. He's one of three people in all eight Great Powers who have completed The Path. He alone stops any attempts. And his presence will continue to do so until he ascends to the higher planes."

"How can one man do that? It seems like they could just send a squad of Tier 40s or stronger." That didn't make sense to Matt, and he refuted the claim. Duke Waters was a legend, but how could one man do so much.

"That isn't allowed."

Seeing Matt's surprise, Griff laughed for real this time. "Yeah, I thought the same thing. Wars are only fought with people Tier 15 to Tier 35. But attacking someone in a lower Tier is forbidden. If a Tier 16 kills a Tier 15, it can domino all the way up to the Tier 50s."

The Tier 15 waved his hand. "If a Tier 40 or higher wants to wipe out all life on a planet, it's *easy*. They could snap their fingers, and we wouldn't know how we died."

Griff leaned back and rubbed his temples. "Twenty or so thousand years ago, a conflict happened where the rules of war were ignored. It was a three-way war between

the eight Great Powers, and someone somewhere killed a battalion of Tier 15s. Then the other side retaliated, getting revenge by sending a team of Tier 17s to kill the Tier 16s. After the war was over, forty-three high Tier worlds were left uninhabitable. Trillions of lives lost. It cost too much to be worth it."

Those numbers and powers were so far out of Matt's realm he couldn't even think about how that would happen.

Griff continued as Matt was thinking, "So, Duke Waters's very presence stops anyone from attacking us and our allies because he's a true monster. He just reached Tier 31, and he can solo Tier 35 rifts. The other two Ascenders are strong but not Duke Waters strong. That's why we have The Path. That's why the Empire allows its best to get killed trying to grow as strong as possible because one man can stop billions of deaths."

He seemed to have aged a dozen years as he leaned forward, putting his weight on his elbows. "And that leads me to Healer Iris. She was a valuable asset to the Empire. Healing skills are rare, and those who wish to dedicate themselves to the profession are even harder to nurture. She lost that value to the Empire after her stunt. If we let people abuse their positions, it breeds enmity. If there isn't a swift punishment, people will do anything they can to take revenge. Just a few years ago, a young man's sister was raped and murdered. He tried to get the culprits punished."

Griff waved off to the side. "He reported it to the authorities and even the nobility of his planet. They ignored him. He was a lower Tiered crafter, and the rapist was a mayor's son. They valued him and his sister

as less because they weren't strong. Do you know what he did to get revenge?"

Matt didn't have words so just shook his head.

"He waited until the city's defensive shielding was up because of a nearby rift break and broke a family treasure. He torched a city of millions. Not a single survivor. It was the only way he could see to right the wrong done to his sister. The Empire has laws for a reason, and when they aren't fairly enforced, millions can pay the cost of a few."

Matt didn't know what to say. It was a grim tale, but one he understood. He had fantasies about getting revenge on the governors and Junipers who let the rift breaks occur. Killing millions seemed excessive in his eyes, but he understood the desire for revenge. That much killing just created more pain.

The room was silent until Griff shook himself, sitting up and slapping his desk. "On to better topics. Matt, you have skill. I've looked at your training stats and clearance rates. You're good. I think you can get to the 10th or 15th Tier safely on The Path. And just that will show our enemies we have one more powerhouse in our rosters they have to be leery of."

He pointed out where Matt thought the accommodations were. "You mentioned Light and Shadow. Do you know why they cover their faces? It's so they don't get assassinated by the other powers. No one wants the Empire to have two sets of Ascenders at once. It would be unprecedented."

The second in command of the PlayPen waved his hands around. "It would make us the strongest power by miles. Duke Waters still has another seven or eight thousand years before he hits Tier 45 and can travel to the higher planes at the fastest. That amount of time is *nothing* to the other seven powers. The mere *thought* of a single Great Power having that kind of power terrifies them. Light and Shadow have probably had an attempt on their lives every few years since they hit Tier 17."

He leaned forward slightly to catch Matt's eyes. "Matt, standing out too much will draw attention. And, yes, you were right. They were weak at Tier 1. It's common knowledge they came from an under Tier 5 world, and so did Duke Waters. As far as which planets they came from? That information is completely hidden. When you roll the dice trillions of times, *that's* how you beat the odds, and *that's* how the Empire gets lucky enough to have two sets of Ascenders."

His eyes were hard but not unkind. "War is close, Matt. Remember this. If you kill a genius before they can fully grow up, they aren't a genius."

Griff stood and walked to the window, peering out at the sun as it peaked over the ocean, bathing the island in the light of the new day.

"To happier topics, what pet did you get? It's obviously ice-based, but did you get something crazy like an ice dragon?"

"No, an arctic fox."

"Ahh, that's still a good one. It starts a bit weaker than a dragon or a phoenix, but all bonds can get to absurd power levels. Hmmm, I don't think we even have bond collars here." The older man nodded along as he spoke.

"Bond collars? I didn't see anything about needing a collar."

Griff glanced at him. "Yup. It's how bonds and pets show they are owned and not just wild monsters until they gain enough intelligence to use an AI. Also, they function like the bracelets and will allow you to share essence. I'll get one special ordered for you."

Griff turned and stuck out his hand. "Matt, really, thanks for coming by. I still am sorry I snapped at you, but I appreciate you for understanding what's at stake."

Then Griff laughed. "Let's hope you get a female fox."

"What? Why's that, Griff?"

Griff just laughed harder. "All nonhuman monsters can take a human shape at Tier 15. Considering you're going to be binding your spirit to your fox, they will be taking a form you find attractive. Marriage between bonds isn't unheard of even if rare."

The older man grinned lecherously. "And, besides, if it's a she, she would be *foxy*."

Matt walked into the general store and looked at his pad. He had a list of things to get, but every time he thought of his fox bond, Matt couldn't help but remember Griff's bad joke.

Griff's wife had walked in at the end of the conversation just in time to hear his ill-timed joke, and a whispered argument ensued. She told Griff if he got an animal companion, she'd have to get a male companion of her own.

Matt felt the argument was strange because she had their child in a carrier the whole time. He was just glad

the kid was asleep when he made his escape and heard the contents of Griff's desk clatter to the floor.

It wasn't like he could change the gender of the animal in the egg. It just seemed weird to want to have sex with something that was once an animal. He pushed the thought off. That was a problem for decades in the future at the earliest. Tier 15 was just a dream to the current him.

Griff had ordered a collar for Matt as an apology, and while Matt felt guilty accepting when he saw the price tag of a Tier 5 mana stone, his protest died.

That was more than twenty-five times his credit limit. Griff warned him that bonds were usually only bought at Tier 5 because they were so expensive. The spiritual strain the bond placed on the cultivator was only a problem if the bond wasn't willing to bond.

The true barrier of having a bond on The Path was the restriction on outside financial assistance for their upkeep. Griff even admitted he was skirting the rules pretty heavily with his 'apology.'

Arriving at the general store, he found an employee who helped him access the off-world catalog Griff had directed him to. The prices were absurd. A month's supply of food for an arctic fox kit cost a little more than a thousand credits.

Matt looked at the egg and wanted to cry. He didn't know how he was going to feed the little monster.

Then there were the toys and bedding.

Why do toys cost hundreds of credits each? Why does the bedding cost four thousand?

As he looked into the blatant extortion, he found pets were considered monsters for a good reason. At Tier 1,

most could chew through iron. All their toy materials needed to be Tier 3 monster parts or higher.

The bedding was specially made for cold creatures and would deflect their cold back at them, which was apparently important. Despite his best efforts, Matt couldn't find any specifics as to why, just that every bed rated for the foxes came with it, and that feature increased the price considerably.

To make matters worse, the fox would also need special alchemical concoctions to strengthen its innate cold powers as they advanced if he didn't live in a high Tier world with significant ice caps.

Matt could see his future of living with no savings and his debt constantly climbing. The only reassurance he had was his peak Tier 1 status after the rift challenge. Now, he just had to wait for his spirit to acclimate to its newfound bond before attempting the breakthrough into Tier 2.

Confirming the purchase for six months of food, two supplement packages, a bed, and a massive number of toys and grooming supplies was painful. Seeing his credit limit instantly halved, Matt almost wished Griff would yell at him again so he could get some more free stuff. If it wasn't for Griff's generosity, he wouldn't have two credits to rub together.

The arrival time for his order was scheduled for two days from now, the quick turnaround being another perk of getting on Griff's bad side. He was grateful he wasn't charged with the usual fee of a Tier 8 mana stone to activate the portal off schedule.

Matt decided to go to the gym to work out. He needed an outlet for his frustration at his newly acquired pauper status, and the only way to claw his way out again was to delve higher Tier rifts.

Tier 2, here I come.

The night before the pet items arrived, Matt was in the shower, pondering the impending arrival of this creature that would have a heavy influence on the rest of his life. The frozen egg left an un-fogged section in the mirror next to it as it rested in the sink next to his shower.

Suddenly, a powerful jolt reverberated in his spiritual energy, warming and chilling him all at once. There was only one thing this bizarre sensation could possibly mean.

His fox was about to hatch.

Matt hastily ended his shower, threw on his pants, and sent a rushed message to Melinda's team.

He was staring at the egg placed carefully on the center of his bed when all six of them barged into the room. Seeing they hadn't missed the culminating moment of their days spent in anticipation, the team sighed in relief.

Less than fifteen apprehensive minutes later, a crack appeared with a crisp, satisfying, ringing sound. The egg shook slightly as the crack expanded along its surface until, finally, the eggshell fragmented into frost-covered pieces.

Out popped a fuzzy mass of white. She, as the hatchling had clearly asserted through their newly formed spiritual

connection, looked at Matt as she wobbled to him on unsteady legs.

The little fox advanced all of three steps before falling over, and Matt quickly scooped her up and cradled her to his chest.

She was so soft. And as frigid as a block of ice. A chill permeated the air around her, emanating constantly from her fur.

He could barely make out sounds of appreciation and wonder coming from the others. Words like adorable, fluffy, and cuddly barely registered. He was completely lost to his surroundings, except for this new facet of his very identity.

Matt only had eyes for the small creature in his arms. Her eyes were squeezed shut, and she seemed perfectly content to stay pressed against his chest, listening to his heartbeat, but she explored the link between their spirits.

It didn't feel as if it was an invasion into his consciousness but, instead, like a hopeful inquiry from an innocent child. Matt got the sense this bond was deeply familiar to her, and the very reason she had woken from her deep sleep. It wasn't through spoken word that he understood her but, instead, he almost immediately interpreted the emotions, colors, and impressions she projected to him mentally.

The tiny kit opened intelligent, light blue eyes the color of towering glaciers. After a few minutes, Matt realized he had forgotten something important.

She was hungry, and she wanted food *now*. He had no idea what he should feed the hatchling. The food he had purchased wouldn't arrive until the next morning.

The dilemma was solved for him, and through the spiritual connection, Matt got an impression of the fractured pieces of egg. Setting her down next to the remains of her vessel, the arctic fox ate half of the remains before falling over, stuffed and exhausted.

Matt looked to the others and saw Melinda biting her knuckles to keep quiet, and the rest weren't faring any better.

His new bond would be asleep for a while, so he whispered, "If you want to pet her, go ahead. She's going to be dead to the world for a while."

That started a very fierce but careful rush to gently stroke her soft fur.

Only now did Matt understand why arctic foxes were prized for their aesthetic more so than their combat ability. Their coats were divine to the touch. The fluffy tail felt how clouds looked.

After they had their fill of admiring and appreciating the new life before them, each member of the party reluctantly left, one after the other, allowing the newly bonded pair to sleep.

Matt woke up the next morning and quickly realized why the fox beds cost so much. The little bundle of fluff had crawled onto his chest in the night to curl up, nose tucked into its tail. But the damn thing had chilled him to the bone as she slept, causing him to wake up shivering.

Gently setting the kit on his pillow, he scurried into the shower, letting the heat wash away the deep chills that permeated his body. Before he had fully warmed himself, he felt a jolt of pure panic through their spiritual link as the kit woke, frantically searching for her lost bond.

Following their connection as it led her to the bathroom door, Matt sensed her irritation as she scratched at the door, worry flowing into his spirit. Stepping out of the water, he bent down to comfort the fox, getting pawed at and scolded with small yips for leaving her side.

The kit left to explore the bathroom, so he finished his shower. She seemed interested in but wary of the falling water. Curiosity overcame her caution as she stuck a paw into the running stream of water. Matt finished up and checked his pad for the status of the delivery.

To his relief, it was at the island's post office waiting for pickup.

Quickly, he scooped up his fox, receiving loud protests to the interruption of her exploration. Matt noted she had finished the egg remains he had left on the side table. Through their link he felt that, while she wasn't hungry, she wasn't full either.

Hurrying down to the post office was a challenge. His fox squirmed in his arms as she tried to take in anything and everything they passed as they went. He quickly grabbed a single bag of kit chow, as well as the box containing the toys and care products. Seeing his predicament, the postal workers didn't make a fuss at him leaving five large bags of food.

When he got back to his room, he found Melinda, Sam, and Tara waiting. Seeing the fox awake, they quickly showered the kit with affection, completely ignoring him and his precariously carried packages.

The little traitor basked in the pets and coos from the girls while Matt unboxed the bowls he had bought and filled one with water, the other with food.

The fox leaped off the girls' laps, darting to the food and scarfing down the kit chow. It was some blend of fish and beef according to the packaging and was supposedly formulated for her breed in particular.

Mathew, Vinnie, and Kyle arrived with breakfast as the fox was still eating, relieving Matt's gnawing hunger.

"Have you decided on a name yet?" Tara asked through a mouth full of food.

"Not yet. I ha—"

"How could you? Are you neglecting her?"

"She's adorable. How could you leave her without a name?"

"Look at her! Call her Snowball."

Vinnie's suggestion started a chorus of clichéd snowy names being suggested while the fox in question just nosed the box of toys. She pulled one out, giving it a shake and a scratch before going back to pull out the next.

"I am not naming her Little White. Why would I put little in her name anyway? She will grow up. And naming her based on her color seems lazy. I'm sure there are a hundred arctic foxes named Snowflake or something similar."

Matt put the supplies for the fox in a bag, and when he got to the collar, he was afraid the fox would resist the small band. However, she didn't seem to mind it at all. She was far more interested in the brush Melinda had found and was using to her growing satisfaction.

The trip down to get the remaining bags of food was even slower. The fox demanded to be let down so she could inspect every new object or stimulus she came across.

Matt found it adorable that she would find something, then push her curiosity to him through their bond as if to ask, 'ohh, what's this?' He would try to explain with vague impressions, but the little ball of fluff didn't have the attention span to allow Matt to get the idea across.

How do you explain what a rock is to a baby?

The fact that everyone who saw the little white fox had to stop and pet her delayed the group even further. The fox loved the attention, and Matt swore she was prancing after a while. That is, until she was distracted by something else.

The slitted eyes of the kit were drawn to a spider, which had built an elaborate web in a nearby bush. The staring match only ended when the kit sneezed, blowing the spider away and startling everyone, including the fox. She shot Matt an inquisitive stare, as if to question 'who did that to her' through their link.

Matt found himself with endless patience. A week ago, if someone had told him he would watch a baby fox take an hour and a half to make the typically much shorter trip to the post office, he would have laughed at them.

Now, curiosity flowed across their bond, and trust in the fact he would keep her safe as she stuck her nose into everything she could reach.

The display led Matt to picture a hazy memory of staring at the stars one night with his parents. The details were lost to him, but the sensation of their care and love was still clear. He remembered asking them the names of each constellation and their patient answers to his repetitive questions.

An idea for a name popped into Matt's head. He looked up and saw bright blue skies but still imagined the stars hidden behind the veil of blue. He smiled and sent a query to his fox.

　　She liked it.

　　Aster liked her name.

CHAPTER 9

Matt was still trying to get used to Aster. She felt the need to be a part of every single thing he did. While it was adorable and cute, it could be frustrating at times.

Currently, he was on his bed, attempting to break through to Tier 2. Every time he sunk into the meditative state required, Aster shifted on his chest, or flicked her tail, or did something else to break his concentration.

He didn't want to fail the breakthrough. It wouldn't harm him, just waste his hard-earned essence. His physical side of cultivation was full, and he had a decent amount of essence in his spirit. He just needed to use that essence to compress the loose essence acquired from delving into something more solid.

The guide suggested a mental image of sand to sandstone, but he felt Aster shift again. Her chill permeated his shirt, his mental imagery shifting to snow being compacted into ice sheets.

From shifting and unstable to firm and unmoving.

With this new place to build upon, the Tier advancements after this would compress his essence even more, slowly adding more weight. This new arrangement of essence would be the foundation the rest of his life would be built upon.

Matt thought of his helplessness after the rift break, and his anger at Iris trying to steal Aster. He took all that emotion and, with every ounce of power his spirit had, he squeezed.

The essence compressed down easily at first as the loose snow became hard. Matt didn't let up. He kept pushing, and just when it felt there was no more progress to be made, the essence compressed again. The once hard bundle of essence he had created shrunk, but it had also loosened. It was only slightly harder than it had started before the first compression.

He repeated the process four more times, five compressions being good for Tier 1. Coming out of his trance with Aster's wet and cold nose against his chin was a bit of a shock.

Matt checked his physical cultivation. Right in the center of his chest was a small, rock hard sphere of essence with a small layer on top that wasn't as densely compacted as its core. Diving into his being with his spiritual sense, he inspected his metaphysical half. The mana cultivation was tiny and seemed atrophied in comparison to his physical half.

Where one was a bright ball of essence, the other was dark and hollow.

He sat up and cradled the kit. Five compressions. He had five more to go to fully stabilize his cultivation, but he'd do it with the first essence he accumulated at the Tier 2 rift instead of allocating it to his core like normal.

That way no problems could occur. Problems were said to be rare, but he didn't want to take chances.

The importance of compressing the essence foundation was repeated numerous times in the guide the PlayPen provided. It was possible to advance to the next Tier with only a single compression, but the cultivator would be able to express less power than their peers who had completed the full ten. Though, apparently, more than ten compressions were possible, but the benefits were negligible, under a tenth of a percent with the returns diminishing with each additional compression.

Still, with his now denser essence, he had officially reached Tier 2.

Tier 2! He had done it.

Aster, feeling his excitement, wiggled out of his hands and picked up a toy. So, Matt played with his bond until she was panting, ready for a nap.

With Aster curled into a chilly ball next to him, he looked up the information of the Tier 2 rift.

It was a jungle path with large insects as the monster of choice. The regular monsters were a mix of giant centipedes with a monstrous bite strength and giant praying mantises with steel-like, grasping arms used as blades and crushers all in one.

The boss was a peak Tier 2 ant queen. Like normal ant queens, this one was a fighter and would ferociously defend her territory. The final fight was against her and a horde of soldier ants.

It was reportedly a hard fight for solo fighters. The only benefit was that the soldier ants were barely Tier 2 and should have trouble getting through his [Cracked Phantom Armor].

The skill was only strong enough to fully block the weakest of Tier 2 attacks, so his advantage was gone. He would slowly be able to get more defensive power out of the skill as it imprinted into his spirit but, for now, he would have to be careful of injuries in the Tier 2 rift.

If his Tier 3 Talent didn't change his mana shortage, he would have to face the fact that the skill would become increasingly less effective.

Matt looked at the snoring fox next to him and was more concerned with her safety. He'd need to bring her with him so she could gather essence as well, but he wasn't sure how to keep her safe from a bunch of ground-level insects.

Maybe I should keep running the Tier 1 rift until she gets stronger?

He decided to ask Melinda's party tonight at dinner. They had actual experience running the Tier 2 rift, and he didn't want to have to run the Tier 1 unless he had to. The Tier 2 monsters would have higher Tier essence, and larger amounts of it at that. Aster would progress and catch up to him much faster if Matt stuck with Tier 2 essence as her fuel.

Their advice was so simple Matt should have thought of it. He bought a larger backpack and stuck Aster inside with a blanket to pad it out for her.

He was sure he looked comical. A man covered in ghostly blue armor with a shield, ax, and a white fox poking her head out over his shoulder.

Even the ant queen was only slightly over waist height, so Aster was out of reach.

Matt worked his way down the main path of the rift, smashing the tough chitin exoskeletons of the monsters. He crushed them one by one as they swarmed him, careful to avoid their mandibles and arms. As he progressed, he barely made out the end of the long trail cut out of the dense jungle foliage surrounding him.

The Tier 2 rift wasn't really any more challenging if he was careful. There were no distinct rooms like the Tier 1 rift. Here, the insects were more ambush predators, focusing more on surprise attacks from the underbrush alongside the jungle path than on frontal assaults.

Matt had tested his limits and had found that his [Cracked Phantom Armor] was nearly impenetrable by singular attacks from the basic monsters. It took them a few seconds of sustained bites or grabs to overcome the mana running through the skill.

As he chopped his way through the waist-high monsters, he eagerly collected the essence. It was weird to describe, but it felt thicker than that of the Tier 1 rift. The difference between water and syrup but less exaggerated.

Splitting a portion with Aster didn't affect his gains as he anticipated. He still seemed to be gathering more essence from each kill here than he would from any two of the Tier 1 monsters, but the space he needed to fill in his core was more than ten times as large as he had needed to reach the peak of Tier 1. Thankfully, Aster seemed to take from a portion he had never noticed he wasn't gathering.

After making his way through the long hot jungle path, leaving a trail of dismembered heads and limbs in his wake, Matt came to a large clearing at the end. Here, the thick underbrush gave way to tall tropical trees and brightly colored flowering plants, all coated with a layer of vines.

In the center of the clearing, a giant mound of dirt signaled the entrance to the queen's underground network of tunnels. As he approached, the ground itself shook and split apart as the queen and her drones breached the surface, sensing the imminent threat.

Sizing up the queen ant, Matt realized he had a problem. She was big, the top of her head reaching slightly above his waist. While he knew her pincer attacks were strong enough to tear him in half, Matt doubted she was fast enough to land an attack.

After quickly dispatching her guard unit, Matt's suspicions proved correct. He easily maneuvered around the queen's slow and predictable lunges, so that wasn't an issue.

The real problem was his inability to damage the queen. His ax didn't have enough weight to drive through the chitin of the stronger insect. Where he could hack and crush the shells of the weaker insects, the queen's exoskeleton was like steel plate armor, and his single-handed ax was ineffective for his purpose.

Matt eventually was able to chop through a weaker leg joint, but all that did was slow her down even more.

Seeing no other viable options, he endured the tedious process of de-legging the queen one limb at a time. Aster, at least, seemed to have a blast yipping at the monster throughout the fight.

The queen's lunging attacks became increasingly pathetic with each missing limb, but he was still wary of her mandible's crushing power. If he was caught in their grip, he didn't think he would escape with all his limbs still attached.

It took him a while, but he was able to separate the queen from her legs and finished the fight by bisecting her at the joints of her head and abdomen.

I'm coming with a bigger ax next time.

Matt approached the reward distortion as he steadied his breathing. This one shimmered with a pale gray light that seemed to try to hide from his sight.

When he collected his prize, he nearly spat at the reward of only four Tier 2 mana stones. A below average haul, which Matt felt summed up the delve perfectly.

The bright side was the bag of mushrooms and herbs he gathered along the forest path. Apparently, they were worth a decent number of credits to the alchemists, so the trip wouldn't be an entire waste.

When Matt checked out and converted his mana stones to credits, he was given a start as the Tier 2 mana stones were worth one thousand credits versus the one hundred of the Tier 1 mana stones. Even with the disappointing amount of mana stones, he still made more in this delve than in four or five average Tier 1 delves.

Arriving at the alchemist workshop, Matt perused the displayed items. Potions of strength, speed, proprioception, and even odder things like night vision littered the shelves in protective casings.

He was disappointed to learn they didn't have actual healing potions, just blood clotting potions. Matt would consider them more alchemical triage than the miracle potions he saw in movies. They were just enough to get you out of a rift and to a healer and little more.

As much as he wanted to get a few of the potions, the problem were the prices. Every item was sold with the price in mana stones. Tier 3 mana stones.

That put the prospect of buying something clear out of Matt's mind, and he gave up on the idea of getting any of the expensive items. Matt left the store area and found a desk with a person behind it to inquire how to go about selling the loot he had from the rift. He told the receptionist he'd like to sell items from the Tier 2 rift and was quickly directed into a back room.

The room he was brought to was occupied by a man in opulent robes. He sat reading a book behind a plan table. Matt sat down and put his bag on the table but was ignored. He coughed slightly to get the man's attention, but the alchemist waved his hand at him with a shushing sound.

After five minutes of waiting, the man put down his book and barked, "Where are the goods?"

After Matt emptied the bag, the man had pulled each item out of the bag and found fault with every single one.

"This one wasn't harvested properly. The entire stem isn't here."

The man rummaged through a few more before saying, "This one has too much surrounding dirt, we can't use this."

How can too much dirt make moss worthless? Frustration building, Matt fought the urge to punch the alchemist in his smug face. The large bag he had trekked through the humid forest was only valued at one hundred credits.

Matt *knew* he was getting ripped off. The guide said the items should have carried a value of fifty credits per item, and the man had a smirk he knew all too well from Benny's. It was the look of someone who knew they were screwing you over and relished it.

Raging internally, Matt thought over what he should do. What irritated him was that he had been careful when harvesting the items. He followed the guide to the letter, so there was no way they were that badly harvested.

Aster, who had sat quietly in her bag, sensed his irritation and started a low growl.

Looking at the smug man across the desk, Matt decided he didn't want this man's money. He wasn't sure if this was a scam the alchemist ran himself or if the entire department was just a bunch of assholes.

Decision made, he snatched the pouch up and stuffed his goods inside. Walking out before the man could say anything, he found a trash can and proceeded to shred every item in his bag.

He got a few odd looks but couldn't tell if they were because of the crazy man angrily tearing up mushrooms and moss, or the fox yipping in excitement every time he did. Matt just wanted to go home and cultivate. That was the only positive he could still hold on to. Finishing solidifying his foundation would be worth the absolute slog this delve had turned out to be.

The next few months of Matt's time on the PlayPen was uneventful. He delved, trained, and took classes when he wasn't relaxing with Melinda's team. Aster also reached Tier 2 and could now push her cold aura out farther, but that ability was useless in actual combat. She had managed to freeze an insect he had cut legs off, which was an improvement, but unless she had actual ice to manipulate, she was limited in her abilities.

She usually just sat behind him, taunting the uncaring insects. But the rifts, while productive, were no real challenge to the duo.

After some time, the day Matt dreaded had arrived. It was Melinda's group's last day on the island. They held a private dinner, and then, the next morning, they would be gone.

It wasn't a surprise that they would be leaving the island before him, but now that the time was here, he didn't want them to go. They were the best friends he had since... Well, he couldn't think of better friends. The other kids at the orphanage all had their own issues that prevented strong friendships from being built. Their shared experiences only made them so close.

He knew it wasn't like they wouldn't be able to communicate; it would just be slow once they were on different planets. The data dumps only happened when the portal was opened, and that was normally once a month. It just felt like he'd be losing them forever.

This was the reason they were leaving two weeks early. Paying for a slot on the monthly portal was only a Tier 3 mana stone apiece, while getting a personal portal was a Tier 8 mana stone.

Sitting on his bed, he cuddled Aster to him. She would be all he had once the others left, and the thought was his only comfort. He didn't even mind anymore that she refused to use the incredibly expensive bed he'd bought her and preferred instead to freeze him nightly. The closeness was nice.

Checking the time, Matt made his way down to the reserved room, with Aster on his heels.

When the duo entered the room, he plastered on a smile he didn't feel. He was determined to act happy to see his friends move on so they didn't feel bad.

As they mostly finished eating, he asked, "So, have you decided where you are going to go?"

"Yup. We've got three jumps to get to the planet. It's called..." Sam looked at her pad, "Relstor. Weird name, but it's a Tier 7 world and has enough Tier 3 and 4 rifts there isn't any real competition for spots. So, no fee to purchase a delve slot, and we can delve as much as we desire."

Matt internally nodded. Planets were able to naturally create rifts with a five Tier range below the planet's own Tier. That meant a Tier 7 planet had Tier 3 through Tier 7 rifts with proportionally more of the lowest Tier of rifts. It was like a pyramid, more Tier 3 rifts and less on up to the planet's own Tier. That same logic was why Lilly had so few rifts. They were missing the bottom level of their pyramid with a Tier 4 planet.

Mathew continued with a full mouth, "There's even a rift with goblins. It's only Tier 3, so just a single tribe.

It's where we'll probably go. It lets us use our numbers pretty well." He swallowed at Melinda's glare before finishing, "And we're familiar with the monster type. We should be able to reach Tier 4 in a few months, give or take."

"That's only if we delve every day, and we talked about that. It's too risky. We're *only* sixteen. We're still well under the curve if our goal is to hit Tier 5 before we reach twenty-two. We don't have to rush for it. The free skill we get at Tier 5 will seriously increase our strength. And, by the way, don't speak with your mouth full, you delinquent," Melinda ended her comment with a poke to Mathew's once again bulging cheek.

Matt agreed, "Yeah, a free skill would be amazing. Do you guys have any idea what you want?"

"Nope. We've only got the two skills among us that aren't Talents. And they were gifts from our sponsor. Have you seen the price for skills?" Melinda was the only one with an empty mouth and answered before she took another bite.

"No, I haven't even looked into them at all honestly."

Tara waved a chicken leg to catch his attention. "Tier 8 rifts are the first point where they become common drops, at around a one in four chance. Even then, it's still only a set number of weaker skills that drop at Tier 8. So, most weaker skill shards sell for about a Tier 8 mana stone."

Vinnie chimed in, "Yeah, but you *can* get lucky and have higher Tiered skills drop. What if we got something like [Regeneration] or a healing skill? That would sell for a lot more."

Kyle cut him off, "Dummy. We'll be the ones *buying* healing skills. Even with the free Tier 5 skill, Melinda's gonna need more healing skills. [Ranged Heal] is great and all, but she needs a group healing skill, and some kind of heal-over-time would be good as well. And [Regeneration] is like Tier 32, so that won't be a free skill for Tier 5s."

Matt understood the bitterness in his voice, so he raised his cup. "To being poor!"

That got a laugh out of everyone, and they started talking about their ideas for archetypes to build into.

Aster took the distraction to steal an extra chicken leg off Matt's plate, and he pretended to not notice.

Matt let the others run with the conversation as his mind drifted. He didn't know what he wanted. It really depended on how his Tier 3 Talent fixed his mana problem. He trusted it would, but he had realized there were multiple ways to 'fix' it, and not all of them would be good.

The best, and most unlikely fix, was his Tier 3 Talent just unblocking his Mana Cultivation. Matt didn't think that would happen, as that would require a direct contradiction of part of his Tier 1 Talent and didn't fit with the growth norm for Tier 3 Talents.

That indecision left him at an impasse he couldn't easily solve. After all, he could hardly make plans if he didn't know what direction his Talent would take him.

He mentally rejoined the conversation to hear Sam say, "I want an area poison skill. It would be so nice. Then I wouldn't have to stab things to actually use my Talent."

That jolted Matt. He had forgotten to check their Talents. The night they met the Emperor was so chaotic with Melinda's Talent, he hadn't remembered to check the others.

Mathew:
- **Talent - Tier 1:** Everyone in the party has lowered threat generation. Threat generation can be redirected to an individual of choice.
- **Talent - Tier 3:** You are much harder to knock off your feet. Being knocked down gives a temporary durability bonus. Grows With Tier.
- **Skills:** None.

Melinda:
- **Talent - Tier 1:** All healing skills are 50% more effective and cost 50% less mana to cast.
- **Talent - Tier 3:** All healing has the 'Overhealth' effect. Grows With Tier.
- **Skills:** [Ranged Heal]

Kyle:
- **Talent - Tier 1:** All strength allocation has double the effect.
- **Talent - Tier 3:** Blood carries extra oxygen, giving strength boost dependent on regeneration. Grows With Tier.
- **Skills:** None.

Sam:
- **Talent - Tier 1:** Poisons and venoms only affect designated targets.
- **Talent - Tier 3:** Can control poisons and venoms in the surroundings if not directly controlled by a skill cast by someone other than Samantha. Grows With Tier.
- **Skills:** [Venom Strike]

Vincent:
- **Talent - Tier 1:** Innate [Earth Manipulation].
- **Talent - Tier 3:** Can see through earth. Grows with Tier.
- **Skills:** [Earth Manipulation]

Tara:
- **Talent - Tier 1:** Innate understanding of ranged weapons.
- **Talent - Tier 3:** Ranged attacks have more penetrating power. Grows with Tier.
- **Skills:** None.

After reviewing the group's Talents, he wasn't surprised but was slightly jealous. They had good Talents, even if they weren't as absurd as Melinda's. The 'grows with Tier' modifier was apparently a ubiquitous trait of Tier 3 Talents.

From what Matt read, Tier 1 was unique, Tier 3 was growth, Tier 25 was power, and Tier 50 was sovereign.

Matt couldn't find much on what the last two actually meant, but they must be powerful to be awakened at such high Tiers. He had heard of more than one account of people becoming powerhouses after being unknowns before their Tier 25 Talent.

He put the pad away, forcing himself into the conversation and to be happy for his friends.

It was five months after Melinda's group left when Matt found himself in trouble. He was slightly surprised it had taken so long.

The new groups of non-sponsees had come with the graduation of the latest year of classes and newest batch of awakenings. Most of them were arrogant but kept it contained to their peer groups. Some pecking order had been established based on their backers he wasn't aware of. Add to the fact most weren't stupid enough to mess with Tier 2 or 3s, so Matt was mostly left alone.

With hundreds of people, one or two were bound to be stupid. And, sadly, Aster attracted stupid.

Matt ate at a table by himself with only his bond. Jasmine, his not so serious girlfriend, was delving tonight, which left him and Aster to eat alone.

Their relationship had started as a physical fling when they encountered each other at the nightly parties' various groups held. That repeated a few times until they

had decided they were a good enough match to make it exclusive while they were at the PlayPen.

As they were eating, someone tapped his shoulder. From the force of the tap, he knew it wasn't anything good, and he debated ignoring them but finally gave up on that idea when he was tapped again.

When he turned, he was confronted by six people. They crowded him and his table, having moved in uncomfortably close. Matt didn't need to be a mind reader to know they didn't have good intentions.

"Do you need something?" He didn't bother being polite. Their demeanor raised Matt's hackles. Even Aster felt the rising tension and looked up from her bowl of food.

He scanned them with his spiritual sense as he waited for their response. They were a group of middling Tier 1s with smirks on their faces.

From just that observation, it was no surprise when the boy in the front said, "Give me that fox. It will make a good gift to my mother."

Matt clenched his jaw so hard he was afraid his teeth would break. "No." He turned around and picked up his utensils, ready to eat.

"You dare to defy me, the son of—" Once Matt heard that, he tuned the idiot out. They could use that kind of pressure on their peers, but there was no larger backer than the Emperor, so he ignored them.

He didn't think they were dumb enough to try and steal from a Tier 2 who was near the peak of the Tier.

Matt decided to let them bluster all they wanted. It wasn't worth the trouble a confrontation would cause.

Sadly, they lacked the sense to quit while they could.

A slap on his shoulder made Matt turn around again.

"Did you not hear me? I—"

Matt faced his dinner again, growling, "Fuck off, kid. No one cares. I'm trying to eat, so go bother someone else."

That's when someone reached for the still eating Aster.

Matt pinned the person's hand to the table with the knife he had been eating with. Rage fueled his actions more than logic, and he let it empower him. He jumped up, shoving his chair back while activating [Cracked Phantom Armor]. The two hits on his back were ignored as he smashed his armored fist into the closest face.

He grabbed the hand holding the dagger that had just skittered down his chest and slammed his palm into the elbow. His assailant crumpled to the floor screaming as Matt moved to kick the nearest person.

Before the fight could escalate further, the guards were on the scene. They had their batons drawn and shouted for everyone to stop.

Matt complied, raising his hands.

One of them barked at him, "End the skill."

Calmly, he replied, "Once the idiot next to me doesn't have a dagger in his hand. I'd rather not get stabbed."

The guard grabbed the kid and his dagger, so Matt deactivated his skill and was pulled off to the side.

Aster hadn't even stopped eating, confident Matt would protect her.

Matt wasn't even mad at her. She didn't do anything wrong by existing. The jackasses shouldn't have tried to steal what was his. He corrected himself, they shouldn't have tried to steal a sentient bond.

Shame the guards arrived so fast or I might have been able to break a few more bones.

His anger at the arrogance they showed still burned like embers in his gut. Matt calmed enough to remove the snarl from his face.

Maybe I'm not as over Iris's attempted theft of Aster as I thought.

He hoped this would teach the fools a lesson, but he doubted it. Paying attention to the detained group, their obnoxious leader prattled on. With a now bandaged hand, he spun a tale of how Matt had stolen their fox, and then fought them.

Idiots.

Aster was well-known and unique. Matt just smirked as the guard asked, "And *that's* your official statement?" before typing in his pad.

Matt honestly couldn't believe the kid didn't realize the guard was letting him dig his own grave.

"See? My fox loves me!"

The idiot reached for Aster with his good hand. If he had been looking, he would have seen her tilt her head. As it neared her, she lashed out, sinking teeth that could tear apart iron, deep into his hand.

The boy let out a guttural scream and wrenched his hand out of her mouth, further shredding his hand.

He then turned to Matt, shouting, "How dare your beast attack me? I'll be wearing it as a coat! And I'll see you hanged for attacking me. My father is the castellan of the Junipers, you worm."

Matt had to replay the words to make sure he had heard the kid correctly.

Confirming he had, he decided to rub salt in the wounds, "Wait? You are the son of a guy who *worked* for the nobles who just. Got. Arrested. And you're flaunting that? Really?"

Matt turned to the table watching the developing drama next to him. "Hey, you! My dad just got canned. Respect my authority!"

As they laughed at his mockery, the kid lunged at Matt but was held back by the guard. He was actually snarling. The crazed display made Matt wonder if the last of his brain cells had short-circuited at the mockery.

Matt sent a thought to Aster, and she snarled at her attempted foxnapper. The blood on her muzzle and large canines made it a far more menacing sight than the kid's attempt had been. The fool flinched back from the fox wearing his blood.

That got even more sniggers from the watchers.

The guard bandaged the kid's other hand, then put him in handcuffs.

"What are you doing? You should be arresting him!"

"Sir, you admitted to a crime not moments ago. And we've already reviewed the security footage. You came to his table and started the confrontation. If nothing else, you lied on an official statement."

The guard read him his rights, but the boy continued to refute the guard's words as he was frog marched away.

After giving his own statement and being asked to wait, a separate guard came over to Matt half an hour later. "You're clear but, in the future, please, don't use so much force."

He just thanked the man and assured him he would be more careful if something like this happened again. He hoped it didn't. Those assholes had ruined his dinner.

Grabbing a meal to go, Matt went back to his room to find Jasmine sprawled across his bed. Aster tried to go and greet the girl, but Matt forced her to sit still while he

brushed her teeth. He didn't know where the foxnapper's blood had been.

Set free, Aster jumped on the bed and shoved a cold nose into Jasmine's cheek, waking the girl up.

"Aster, nooooo! It's so cold."

Aster cuddled in deeper. Then licked the brunette's face.

"Why does your breath smell minty? Did you eat poop again?"

Aster looked heartbroken, utterly betrayed at the mention of her past folly.

Jasmine opened her eyes and saw the food Matt bought as he left the dining hall.

"Oh, you brought me food! You're the best." With a sweet smile and a quick kiss, Jasmine stole his dinner and started digging in.

In between bites, she asked, "So, why did you brush Aster's teeth? Did she really eat poop again?"

Aster yipped her protest. She had only done it once after all and, really, it wasn't her fault. She hadn't known what it was.

Matt told the story, and Jasmine was in disbelief that he had been accosted. When she heard the part that he was the castellan's son she just ahh'd.

"Yeah, I met him a few times. Always acted like his father was the biggest backer one could have. The funny thing is, most kids from the Junipers his age *hated* him. Never understood how he was so arrogant."

She swallowed another bite. "Whatever. *Maybe* before he could have gotten his father to put some pressure on you, but now he's got nothing. From what I heard, the workers of the Junipers were all given one free pass to the

PlayPen so they wouldn't fight the transition of power, but that was it."

"I'm not worried, just amazed how someone could be that stupid. He lied to the guard, who repeatedly asked him 'is this your official statement?' Like, he was given so many chances."

Jasmine finished the sandwich, "Well, enough of idiots, I just had an amazing run and we got seventy Tier 2 mana stones."

She bit her lip, then turned around and walked into his shower. "Want to help me celebrate?"

Matt looked up from his bed. Today was the day. His delve was in four hours, and his physical cultivation was nearly full.

It had taken ten months of delving the Tier 2 rift and, finally, only a month shy of his sixteenth birthday, he was about to hit Tier 3. This kind of rapid cultivation was the greatest advantage of a solo delver.

Aster wasn't slowing him down at all. Pet companions could gather essence humans normally couldn't through eating the unrefined monster meat, so she was gathering what he was unable to.

She was at middle Tier 2, and nearly her full size at almost ten pounds and three feet long. She could easily defeat the Tier 2 insects in a one-on-one fight. Her ice powers were still weak, but they got stronger every day.

Since Aster could also eat the monsters and gain essence that way she always did. She relished eating her personal kills, even if the insects tasted horrible to her. The impression he got through their bond was one of pride and victory.

That ability to eat monster meat made Matt jealous. Humans needed specialized chefs to process the food, otherwise the mana and essence in the flesh was extremely toxic. The problem was, no chef would work with monsters under Tier 5. The sheer amount of mana it took to prepare the meat for the cooking process made it not worth their time and resources.

Matt stood and was about to leave to catch the bus to the rift portal when Jasmine opened the door. "Guess what? My parents got me and my team a slot in a Tier 3 rift one planet over and an interview at a guild."

She hugged and kissed him before doing the same with Aster.

"That's good news. I know your team was bummed out that y'all didn't get sponsored."

She frowned at the mention of her team's plight. They were a party of non-sponsees, who had hoped to catch someone's eye and get sponsored before their advancement to Tier 3.

It just never happened, and Matt agreed with their assessment it had a lot to do with the Emperor's recent proclamation. Anyone who had lost family in the unaddressed rift breaks and reached Tier 15 would become the rulers of their home planet, which was an enticing reward for anyone able to sponsor for The Path.

Sponsors were finding and scouting the orphanages around the world according to the news reports Matt saw. They weren't looking to sponsor a team with

wealthy connections who had not suffered during the rift breaks, and thus were not eligible to get the big reward.

Jasmine frown deepened. "That's the problem. The rift is on my dad's home world, and he had to pull strings to get the slot. Which means we have to leave today. The portal is this evening, and we can't leave the slot open for long or we'll lose it."

Matt felt like he had been punched in the gut. Today was his big day. He was going to reach Tier 3, and she had to leave now?

Is there a Tier 50 playing pranks on me?

Matt worked hard to not let his melancholy show.

Jasmine and her team were good people. While they came from rich families, they tried their hardest and never acted arrogantly. When they had heard of Matt's fight, they had all reached out to their parents to make sure none of the others in the castellan son's party tried to make trouble with him.

It had been unlikely with Matt being on The Path, but they had done it simply because Jasmine cared about him despite them both knowing their relationship was one of convenience.

"Well then, good luck and congratulations. It's a big step, I know you guys only had another two months on the island, but it's good to see you have a path forward."

"It's just terrible timing, but I can't make everyone wait on me. I know today is a big day for you. I just wish I could be here with you to celebrate." Jasmine got a look on her face and asked, "You have what? Four hours till your rift?"

At Matt's nod, she pushed him into the room.

"Good. We have time for one last goodbye."

Matt watched Jasmine run out of his room and down the hall, hair still mussed. They had cut it far closer to her boat's departure time than they had planned, but neither could let go.

With a promise that if they ended up on the same planet again, they'd at least say hello, she had left.

There wasn't much either could do at this point. Her path was forward, and Matt's was still on the PlayPen.

Matt went down to the waiting area and sat impatiently. He couldn't stop looking at his pad. Aster had gotten tired of his impatience. She started roaming out of boredom and was sniffing a bush off to the side of the road.

When the bus arrived, Matt held down the urge to push through the exiting people and tell the driver to hurry. He did none of that and waited his turn. Fantasies of finding a teleport skill in his shoe and just teleporting to the rift running through his head.

The ten-minute ride to the rift was the longest of his life.

Entering the rift, Matt hurried Aster into his backpack, and he sprinted through the jungle path.

He would get as much essence from killing the queen ant and her soldier ants as he would get from killing the fodder insects, so he ignored the lesser monsters. He only needed half of the queen's essence to make the attempt at his breakthrough and couldn't bear to wait any longer than he had to.

When he reached the queen's area, he hastily sped past her drones and drove his heavy ax into her skull with an impatience-fueled attack. Only after feeling the rush of essence from the queen did he massacre the remaining ants.

Matt checked his pad. His delve had only taken twenty minutes. If he hurried, he could catch the next bus back to the residential area, where he could perform his breakthrough and test his Tier 3 Talent.

Quickly grabbing the mana stones the reward distortion hid, Matt exited the rift and bypassed the checkout counter, sprinting to the bus stop.

He climbed on and mentally begged the bus driver to leave early.

Aster, pouting in the seat next to him, forced him to calm down.

He didn't like to cultivate when sitting, so he picked Aster up and went to the back of the bus. There were seats running the entire back wall where he could lay down.

Once he was horizontal, he forced his spiritual sight inward.

Calming his breathing, Matt gathered the newly acquired essence in his spirit, wrapped it around his little sphere of physical essence, and squeezed.

What was loose turned hard. What was hard turned solid.

His Tier 1 essence was compressed even further when Matt squeezed his Tier 2 essence down.

One compression, two compressions, three, four, five. It was after the sixth that Matt lost his momentum and couldn't continue.

He felt his physical cultivation with his spiritual sense a second time.

Tier 3.

He had done it.

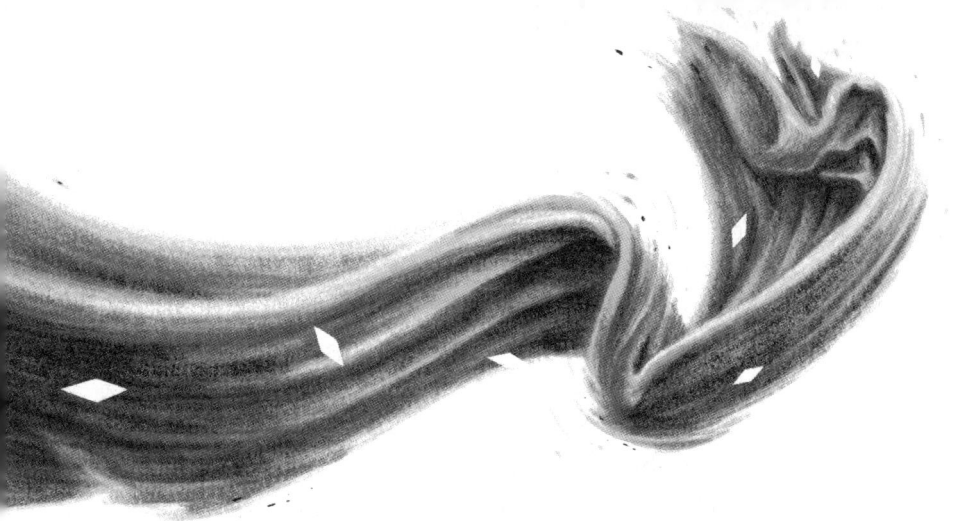

Chapter 10

Matt probed at his mana cultivation and felt it still completely blocked.

It made him panic.

Eric and Dena had told him they believed his Tier 3 Talent would fix his problem. The scanner didn't unlock the Talent, it just analyzed the spirit and deduced what the unique change in the spirit did for the cultivator.

Matt felt at his mana levels and only observed it nearing the 10% mark it usually sat at.

Nothing unusual.

He was tempted to get off the bus and run the way back. The knowledge that it would be slower than just waiting was the only thing that stopped him, but he *had* to get to the scanner.

The next seven minutes felt like decades. He watched each tree passing and urged the driver to just go a little faster. The driver ignored his internal pleading.

Matt did the only thing he could do and moved to a seat right by the middle doors. They would be slightly closer to the training facilities, and he was going to run for it as soon as the bus opened its doors.

Aster didn't care for his impatience. She pushed thoughts he interpreted as 'what's done is done. You can't change your Talent, so calm down.' Matt knew she was right, but he had been looking forward to this moment since Miles had given him hope the day of his Tier 1 Awakening.

The bus stopped, and Matt ran, Aster yipping at his heels.

Once inside the testing room, he quickly sat down and placed his arm into the tube and tapped on the pad to start the Tier 3 Talent scan after bringing the second bar over his chest.

Time seemed to slow as the machine whirled and hummed. As the moments passed, Matt was hyper aware of a bead of sweat that wandered its way down his back.

Any movement was impossible. He had to remain still for the machine to get a good scan of his spirit, and if he moved and slowed this down, he would need to repeat it. If that happened—

> **Tier 3 Talent determined.**
> **Primary Effect:** Any mana in the mana pool over the maximum will permanently increase Maximum Mana.
> **Secondary Effect:** Maximum Mana can at most double from the previous maximum, once per Tier.
> **Tertiary Effect:** Maximum Mana adjusted to unknown value.

Matt read the readout twice and laughed hysterically. The Talent was useless. He couldn't regenerate any mana over 10% without decades of time.

As an idle thought passed through Matt's mind, he shot out of his chair and started running to the general store. Aster sent confused thoughts and yips as she followed him.

A small kernel of hope bloomed in his chest. He wanted to smack himself. He might not be able to regenerate to full, but he could store mana in a refillable mana stone. Then he just had to draw it back into himself to fill his mana over his usual max to meet the conditions of his Talent.

He had done so for Melinda, which was the thought he had had.

Their group had bought their healer twenty rechargeable mana stones. They had gotten the expensive ones that allowed the user to inject a sample of their own mana, and the stone would slowly convert any mana added after into mana with that aspect.

They had done it so Melinda wouldn't run out of mana in a rift. So long as she had mana, she could make them effectively immortal, so keeping her topped off was their priority.

The problem was, even with all their Mana Regeneration stats, it would take days of putting their mana into the stones to fill them. Each stone could hold 200 mana, with twenty stones, they would need 4,000 mana. So, they had decided to wait before delving new rifts without the mana stones full as a safety measure.

If Melinda didn't fill the rechargeable mana stones herself, she would need to wait for the mana to un-aspect into ambient mana, then aspect to match her mana. It would take a week per cycle and using the mana from low Tier mana stones was just too expensive to justify. So, the team was going to spend their mana, but the ones with skills wouldn't be able to practice, which was less than ideal.

There were better stones that let you spend more mana to speed the process up, but their price started at Tier 15 mana stones. For the largest capacity of 200 mana, it was a Tier 25 mana stone. The group had no way to borrow that amount of money so were stuck with the slower stones.

Matt had offered to fill them for the group, and what would have taken them days had taken him a little over an hour, though Melinda would still need to wait for the mana to convert to her personal mana. It didn't cost her team their mana.

It was why he knew his idea was possible. The mana he gave Melinda remained his mana, so he was able to reabsorb it without issue.

As he arrived at the general store, he ran to the wall that held the rechargeable mana stones and the chargers. The middling grade ones like Melinda's group had bought were nearly a million credits, but he passed them by without a second look. That was mostly because of their aspecting ability, and because the efficiency ratio was over 90%.

Matt didn't need either of those features, so he moved to the back where the cheaper versions were shelved. He found the cheapest model for just ten thousand credits and checked the back of the packaging information.

It was a pretty crappy model with an efficiency ratio of barely 20%, but Matt had mana to spare. He didn't mind if he lost mana while charging the stone.

Flipping the package, he scoured the back of the box for information about the mana stone sold with the charger. He found it. It was a cheap mana stone that only had a max capacity of 50 mana and couldn't aspect the mana inside.

It was perfect. At least, it was perfect for Matt to test on.

On his way to the counter, he grabbed a cheap handheld scanner that would allow him to check his maximum mana and current mana. He had never bothered before because all cultivators could feel how full their mana pool was at any time, but that was a ratio not a hard number.

He couldn't increase his mana so why get something to show him a number less than one?

After checking out, Matt found a tree outside, sat down, and tore into his purchases.

The scanner went on his wrist, and he checked the display.

> **Mana: 0.1/1.0**

Matt picked up the charging system for the rechargeable mana stone and slotted it. He directed mana into the device and felt the waste of mana caused by the 20% efficiency. Most of the mana dissipated into the air, lost to the planet.

He waited. Watching the number climb.

> **Current Mana: 1**
> **Current Mana: 2**

Shaky hands pulled the stone out and absorbed the mana.

> **Mana: 2/2**

Matt laughed. He laughed till tears streamed down his face.

He had done it. He had made it to Tier 3, and his Talent did what Dena and Eric had predicted it would.

Finally, he could increase his mana. It wasn't perfect like cultivation of mana would have been, but it was a start. He could make this work.

Matt pulled the worried Aster into a hug and sent happy thoughts through their bond. She responded by cleaning the salt off his face.

After he collected himself, he filled the mana stone to five mana. It was amazing to feel the stone fill even faster. With his under 1% Mana Regeneration being equal to his Maximum Mana, he could now output double the mana he had a moment ago.

> **Mana: 5/5**

Matt repeated the process again, giddy with anticipation.

> **Mana: 10/10**

Repeating the process for a fourth time, he charged the stone to twenty mana but, this time, nothing happened. The mana over ten just refused to expand his Maximum Mana.

He sent his awareness into his mana cultivation side and looked at the once dark core. It was now vibrant. Not as large or bright as his physical core but alive. A quick test showed he still couldn't add essence, but he hadn't expected it to work.

It was odd that his mana stopped at ten and not some other number like four or eight, as if his Talent was acting retroactively, but Matt threw that thought to the back of his mind.

Neither thing bothered him. He felt like he'd float off if he got any happier. He pulled out his pad and did some math. The Talent reader said it would double each Tier. He wanted to visualize what his projected Maximum Mana would be, and what he could expect to regen in between fights.

His Mana Regeneration under 1% of his total mana was equal to his Maximum Mana, and that number was important, so he made a column for that. His regeneration rate fell off quickly after passing the 1% mark, but he could accumulate 10% of his maximum mana in ten minutes if he accounted for the decrease in his regeneration. And his Maximum Mana was his mana regeneration rate as long as he was under 1%, so it was good to see on the chart.

That was a reasonable timeframe in between fights, and with that small reserve, he'd be able to get a spell off at the start of a fight. He made a column for that as well.

His current mana at 1% would be important in the higher Tiers. He would always have that much mana, so it was good to at least figure out what his numbers would be. If that number was higher than the initial cost of a spell, he could cast that spell with no cooldown other than the skills cooldown.

Setting up the formulas, he made a chart to Tier 25.

Tier	Max Doubles To	10% of Max	1% of Max
Tier 1	1	0.1	0.01
Tier 2	1	0.1	0.01
Tier 3	10	1	0.1
Tier 4	20	2	0.2
Tier 5	40	4	0.4
Tier 6	80	8	1
Tier 7	160	16	2
Tier 8	320	32	3
Tier 9	640	64	6
Tier 10	1,280	128	13
Tier 11	2,560	256	26
Tier 12	5,120	512	51
Tier 13	10,240	1,024	102
Tier 14	20,480	2,048	205
Tier 15	40,960	4,096	410
Tier 16	81,920	8,192	819
Tier 17	163,840	16,384	1,638
Tier 18	327,680	32,768	3,277
Tier 19	655,360	65,536	6,554
Tier 20	1,310,720	131,072	13,107
Tier 21	2,621,440	262,144	26,214
Tier 22	5,242,880	524,288	52,429
Tier 23	10,485,760	1,048,576	104,858
Tier 24	20,971,520	2,097,152	209,715
Tier 25	41,943,040	4,194,304	419,430

Matt looked at the numbers in disbelief, then checked his math for a second, then a third time.

His stomach churned, and he wanted to vomit. These numbers were absurd. At Tier 25, he would have a reserve of 400,000 mana to cast spells from and was unable to go lower.

There wasn't public information for high Tier mages, but Matt didn't think that most of them would have a Maximum Mana of 40 million at Tier 25 or a Mana Regeneration of 41,943,040 mana per second.

With trepidation, he continued the graph for the next twenty-five Tiers. Looking at the Tier 50 numbers, Matt could taste the bile in his throat.

He was suddenly glad that he had gotten confirmation from the Emperor himself that no one could see Talents.

Tier	Max Doubles To	10% of Max	1% of Max
Tier 50	1,407,374,883,553,280	140,737,488,355,328	14,073,748,835,533

He would be generating one and a half quadrillion mana a second at Tier 50. Matt looked up the mana numbers for higher tier mana stones. That was a Tier 46 mana stone every fraction of a second.

At least at Tier 25, I'll only have a generation of a Tier 24 mana stone an instant.

The panic peaked. Quickly, he erased the chart and deleted the application he had used to make it. He didn't need anyone to know how stupid his mana generation would become. It would be a good way to end up a slave to some Tier 40 plus superpower.

Matt decided right then and there that if his secret ever got out, and he wasn't strong enough to protect himself, he'd throw himself to the Emperor's mercy before submitting to an unknown. He wasn't naive enough to believe the Emperor was a benevolent person, you couldn't rule thousands of worlds, reach Tier 50, and be soft, but he *had* met the man, even if briefly.

If he could treat a lowly Tier 1 with a detrimental Talent with kindness, he probably wouldn't throw Matt into a hole in the ground to charge mana batteries by the millions.

What shocked Matt was how innocently it all started. Conceptually, he understood how doubling worked, but he wouldn't even reach what a normal Tier 1 had in Maximum Mana until Tier 6. By Tier 15, he was pretty sure he'd be caught up with most mages of the Tier and, after that, he'd blow them out of the water.

It gave Matt a lot to think about. He was a melee fighter out of necessity. The minuscule amount of mana he had, and his only skill shard forced his style.

Should I consider changing my fighting style to a magic-based one?

As he thought it over, he decided no. At least not until Tier 8 when skill shards started commonly dropping in rifts. Then he could collect more skills and diversify his combat methods.

Matt thought of the graph. Even then, he would not have enough mana to cast any skill that didn't allow charging.

It wouldn't be until Tier 10 that he could constantly throw out low-cost spells like [Fireball]. That meant he would be a melee fighter for the foreseeable future but, over time, he could slowly transition into a true blade mage in the higher Tiers.

Sitting there under the tree, he imagined it. He would be stronger than most at any given tier, at least physically. Even the craziest melee fighter put at least 15% of their essence into mana cultivation so they could use skills. The fact he could dump all his essence at each tier into

In the movie, he had only killed those who had directly wronged him, but Matt well knew that history was only written by the survivors. If the movie was only half-accurate, Matt understood how the duke alone could hold off the other Tier 50 Great Powers.

The man was as cold as his namesake, and as unforgiving. Matt could easily imagine the duke biding his time until drowning entire planets of any enemy dumb enough to attack the Empire.

Matt wasn't sure how much was propaganda but, in the movie, Waters had repeatedly expressed loyalty to the Empire.

Could the Emperor even stop the duke if he wasn't loyal?

Matt wasn't sure. The Emperor was a Tier 50 powerhouse, but Duke Waters was a known monster. How long until the duke was Tier 50, or even Tier 45? It wouldn't be the first time the duke had killed someone five Tiers above himself.

Could they even make this movie if the duke didn't approve of it?

From what he could find on the EmpireNet about him, the duke was cold, but he upheld the laws of the Empire above all else. The man didn't tolerate people of higher Tiers taking advantage of lower Tiers. Matt wasn't sure if it was a vendetta or a crusade against a past wrong, but the man was brutal to anyone he found.

As he found more information, he saw the duke as more of a protective figure than a monster.

He had recently killed a fellow duke, Duke Cumulus, when it came to light that Cumulus had captured several young women and had kept them in what was described as a "sex and torture chamber."

Waters had killed Duke Cumulus and proceeded to block all attempts of the media from finding the identity of the women involved.

The only information the media had obtained was that they were all under Tier 5. The duke had killed a fellow noble, a Tier 35 noble, over a couple of people under Tier 5.

How many people would value a few Tier 5s over a Tier 35?

He wasn't sure many would. A Tier 35 was a strategic weapon. How many were there in the Empire? It couldn't be that many, maybe a few thousand. Matt thought about that again and changed his mind. There could be a ton. The only way to die after Tier 15 was getting killed, after all, so the number would only increase as time passed.

The only thing slowing down growth after Tier 25 was the lack of rifts available. There were only a hundred or so worlds in the Empire that were over Tier 30. With the capital being the only Tier 47 world in the Empire, the top powerhouses had to share the few Tier 47 rifts.

That made it even more impressive that the Emperor was Tier 50. How long must it take to advance when the essence requirements were that high and there wasn't even a rift of your Tier to delve?

Matt stopped thinking of things far beyond his level and cuddled the block of ice also known as Aster as they drifted off to sleep.

physical cultivation gave him an advantage that would only keep growing as time went on.

A future blossomed in front of Matt. He would be an unkillable tank with [Cracked Phantom Armor] and could throw out siege-level skills without rest.

The fantasy was cut short by Aster's cold nose poking him. She sent over her feelings of hunger and a desire to be brushed as compensation for him ruining her delve today.

He just smiled and picked the large fox up. She struggled, but Matt could feel through the bond how much she loved to be carried and knew how she'd protest if he actually set her down.

As they ate, Matt browsed the classes he'd need to take. One was directed physical cultivation, and the other was called Tier 3 and Beyond Planning for The Path and After. He looked for the next available slots and found that they were held once a week and back-to-back.

Looking deeper, Matt saw they were taught by Griff and Helen on alternating weeks. Helen, he learned, was the director of this PlayPen. He assumed she was the woman Griff had been standing behind when Melinda's group found themselves the center of attention.

Quickly, he signed up for the upcoming class. When he went to request a Tier 3 rift slot as well, he was unable to. He received an error message stating slots would be provided only after the Tier 3 classes were taken.

Matt went back to his room. It felt lonely. The cheer from his Talent and advancement lessened a little.

It still smelled like Jasmine.

Another person who left him.

It was hard not to be resentful at the world. It would have been so much better if he was able to celebrate with her. He knew it wasn't either of their faults, but the empty room almost seemed to mock him.

Curling up with Aster, they watched a movie. Matt pretended he didn't notice her stealing popcorn while she pretended to care about the movie. It was a fair trade all things considered.

He was, at least, entertained. It was the newest movie about Duke Waters's time on The Path.

This movie covered his time as a Tier 15 when he was just becoming famous, and how a guild tried to trap him into a binding contract.

Duke Waters had been chased down, and when he escaped pursuit, he circled around and started killing everyone from the guild responsible for the attack. It took him almost a year, but after that time, the guild was disbanded. Even with a Tier 25 leading the guild, people had been afraid Waters would come for them next.

Matt wasn't sure how much of the movie was real, but it was interesting to see higher Tier combat. The duke got his name for the very element he had dominion over, and it was justly earned.

His ability to summon absurd quantities of water meant he could simply drown his enemies. He, at least in the movie, could breathe underwater and had achieved several kills by hiding in the swampy area the guild was based out of and pulling people into the murky water.

Matt almost felt bad for the guild members Waters killed; their deaths were brutal and slow. Duke Waters locked the water around them, so they could only look back at him while they struggled their last. Drowning with the surface inches above you seemed like a special torture to him.

The next morning, Matt went and trained with his newly increased mana regeneration for some testing. He first went to the skill-testing room and performed the same series of tests he had done when he was a Tier 1 to [Cracked Phantom Armor].

The results were slightly worrying. He could only put about three mana a second into [Cracked Phantom Armor] before the pure amount of mana overwhelmed the structure in his spirit and it destabilized. He had hoped to be able to shove all ten mana a second into the skill and become an unkillable wall, but the skill couldn't handle that kind of mana input yet.

Tripling the mana gave increased results, and Matt was positive he could slowly train the skill to accept more mana through practice. That flexibility and malleability were the benefits of having the skill in his core spirit.

He just needed time.

The results of his testing were promising. At three mana a second, he was completely impervious to Tier 2 attacks, and Tier 3 attacks needed a few seconds to break through. Only multiple, direct attacks to the same location in a short amount of time were an actual threat, while attacks that hit different areas were of little concern.

He could advance either by increasing his mastery with the skill or getting it to accept more mana per second. That would entail slowing forcing the skill to the edge of breaking so it got used to that and would accept that level throughout.

The mastery would happen naturally as the skill burned into his spirit, and he got used to using it. The longer it was nourished by his spirit, the more it would strengthen, and the more power he would get out of the skill for the same cost.

Either way, Matt was happy. He could delve Tier 3 rifts with a level of safety most other delvers without expensive armor couldn't hope to match.

With nothing else to do, the duo went to the gym where he worked out, and Aster played around. He was at loose ends until Friday when he could take the class with Helen and get his Tier 3 rift slot. He wanted to see what he could buy now. He was Tier 3, but the sign-up details of the classes had recommended holding off on any big purchase until after the classes.

Matt really wanted to check out the enchanted swords he now had access to, but he knew the Empire had to have its reasons for its recommendations. It had nurtured billions of Tier 3s in PlayPens, so he trusted their regulations. He just wanted to see the new toys he could play with but avoided temptation by not looking anything up.

The class was in a small room with only enough seats for ten. When Matt arrived, there was no one else there. Checking his pad to make sure he had the time and location right, he sat after confirming he was in the right spot.

Aster had wanted to sleep in, so he left her in his room.

Five minutes before the class was supposed to start, another party of four came in and nodded to Matt before sitting.

At 9:00 a.m. on the dot, Griff walked in.

"Hello. I'm going to be the instructor today. Director Helen had other matters that demanded her attention and could not be pushed off."

He placed his bag next to the desk he sat at and continued, "If you would like to wait and take the class with Director Helen next week, feel free to leave." No one moved. "Well then, let's get started.

"We'll start with directed physical cultivation. It's hidden before Tier 3 for a reason. If a cultivator allocates their essence wrong, they can cripple themselves, so it's better to gain some experience with cultivation first. You can allocate into the seven main categories. They are—" He tapped the air in front of him and the screen behind Griff showed the categories he listed, "strength, durability, proprioception, which is sometimes called dexterity, flexibility, senses, mind, and regeneration.

"That's the most basic level of directed cultivation. At Tier 5, you can go one level deeper. For example, in strength, you can focus on particular muscle groups or types of muscles. In senses, you can increase smell over vision, or vice versa."

The older man shook his head. "It's not recommended to try and reach for that layer yet. It's dangerous because, without the foundation, you can get your abilities out of whack and not be able to function. I wouldn't even recommend it until Tier 15, but at Tier 5 it's safe enough."

One of the girls in the party had a hand raised.

"Just hold the questions for now. I'll probably cover it. If I don't, I'll take all the time we need after to explain. Write it down if you think you'll forget."

He cleared his throat before continuing, "You should never direct cultivate more than 50% of the essence you are going to allocate into your physical core per Tier. If you have too much strength, you can hit hard, sure, but without the proprioception, you won't hit what you're aiming at. Or without the flexibility, you'll pull a muscle every time you reach for something. Without durability, you'll break a bone punching something, and so on.

"50% is a nice, safe margin. Also, if you are going to direct cultivate, it's better to do that *after* undirected cultivation. Undirected cultivation will try to fill in the areas with the least amount of essence allocated before anything else, so it's better to direct cultivate afterwards. A good way to picture it is snow filling valleys more than building up the peaks of mountains even higher.

"Questions before I move on?"

The girl from earlier raised her hand again. "What about mind and regeneration?"

"What about them?" Griff didn't seem to hear a question in the girl's question.

"Well, how do they work? Does mind make you smarter, then? Does regeneration work like the skill?"

"Ah, good question. No and no. Mind will make you think faster, but you won't be 'smarter.' It will just let you process information a little faster. Any ideas are on you. If you want to get smarter, take classes and learn new stuff."

Griff gestured as he said, "Regeneration is just boosting the body's natural recovery. You won't be growing back limbs or anything, but it *will* let your body

adapt to heavy healing better. Also, if you get rich enough to buy [Regeneration], the essence in that portion of the core will multiply the effect of the skill a bit.

"Regeneration is also good for increasing endurance. It will help the muscles recover faster. It's not a replacement for working out and increasing endurance that way, but helps prevent getting tired in a fight.

"Did that answer your question?" the girl nodded.

"Good. Directed cultivation is really useful when you need more of a particular ability for your fighting style. An archer will still want strength to pull a bow, but proprioception and flexibility will be higher priorities. Even senses are useful. Mind and regeneration as well. But that's why I'm telling you not to direct cultivate more than 50% of your allocation. You should only be multiplying your strongest aspects not neglecting the other."

A thought seemed to come over Griff, and he added, "Mind is needed as you get into higher Tiered combat. Monsters will be faster because of their strength, and mind will let you actually process the attacks. I knew a guy who didn't want to 'waste essence in mind,' His logic was that it doesn't help you be smarter so why invest in it? He got his throat slit from an attack he couldn't even react to. He could have defended against it, but he couldn't process the information and react in time. He then spent the next two Tiers fixing that mistake with his allocation. Lucky bastard only lived because we had a healer with us."

One of the guys asked, "What about strength? Why work out at all if a cultivator could just focus on strength some."

Griff nodded. "That's a good question actually. Strength and all physical cultivation multiply what's there. One multiplied by five is just five, but two multiplied by five is ten. Your physical body will allow you to get more power for your essence expenditure.

"If you train proprioception with hand-eye coordination games, you'll see more improvement with the essence you put in. But if you don't train at all, you'll see only minimal benefits.

"That's another benefit of regeneration. It will, around Tier 8 for an average melee fighter, be high enough you won't lose muscle mass by not working out. A nice side benefit."

The last guy in the party spoke up, "But how do you have the time to train all of that?"

"You don't, not really. It's part of the reason The Path is so hard. Most people hit Tier 15 and spend a few years just training and shoring up their weakest points. If you are still on The Path, you don't really have time for that."

Griff looked off into the distance. "That's about it for physical cultivation. Questions before we move on? Information packets will be made available to you on the PlayPenNet after this. They go into more detail if you want to check specific ratios or interactions between parts of cultivation. I suggest you at least skim it over."

No one had any questions, so Griff continued, "Okay, next is what to do now that you're Tier 3 and only have six months left in the PlayPen." He met each of their eyes, "That countdown starts the day you do your first Tier 3 rift, or two weeks after this class."

Matt noted that. He had figured it started from the moment he broke through, but it was good to know his enforced downtime wasn't going to hurt him.

"First thing is planning for when you leave the PlayPen. There is a priority for people on The Path concerning rift slots, and we have a list of all the Tier 3 and 4 rifts on the nearest couple of planets."

As Griff said that, Matt's pad pinged with a second information packet, and he assumed it had the information the older man mentioned.

"Speaking of rifts on other planets, the Tier of the planet shows the highest Tier rift that will form stably on the planet. Usually, a planet will have stable rifts at the Tier of the planet minus five. So, a Tier 10 planet will have five through ten.

"Any lower means someone is preventing it from growing stronger, or it's brand-new and still growing. It's expensive to prevent the growth of a rift, but you'll find it on stronger worlds with developed noble families or strong guilds. They're used for training their own people and aren't usually available for public use."

Griff sighed at that but continued, "But you all have three big purchases in front of you. And they're expensive enough you'll want to choose at least one while in the PlayPen for the discounts."

"First is an enchanted weapon. Getting something with a sharpness and durability enchantment is pretty much all your spirits can handle at this Tier. Well, you can get any one major enchantment and one minor, unless you have an exceptionally strong spirit. Those are the recommended runes to put on bladed weapons anyway."

He raised two fingers in the air. "Second is a personal AI. It takes a core skill slot, but the sooner you get one the better because it grows with you. They are great for everyday general use but, in combat, they are invaluable.

They can provide a HUD, and if you have a party, they can get information from the other AIs about your teammates' physical conditions. So, you can know if they are low on mana or get injured. They will save your asses more often than you can possibly imagine.

"They come with preset builds for the basic types of combat. For the melee versions, they can run predictive algorithms on your opponent. For ranged combat, it can do the same thing, just not as well. Showing wind speed for an archer or tracking opponents is their main job. For mages, it can help spell cost by assisting casting, along with a lesser version of the ranger things."

Griff leaned forward. "The AIs start as a base template and will improve in their specialized aspects over time. You can also get the software for the other versions, so you won't lock yourself out of any capabilities in the future. But the ones you get first will improve more as they have more time to grow. Eventually, the AI will be unique to yourself and good at what you need it to do.

"The downsides are, they're expensive, they reserve more mana with each software running, and—"

That sent Matt's hopes crashing. The AI seemed perfect to him. The predictive capabilities seemed amazing, and that also meant he could use the information gathered for the training rooms instead of paying for the premade versions.

He just didn't have mana to reserve.

"They can eat into your regular mana pool if you make them compute too much. It's mana expensive and, at low Tiers, it can hurt you if you buy too many modules.

"Finally, a spatial bag is a great purchase." Griff pulled a backpack from his ring with a flick of his wrist.

"They're lesser versions of spatial rings. They can hold stuff but don't reduce the weight much. And they don't have the effect of slowing time on the items placed inside. They're still useful, though, so don't think otherwise."

"Your spirit won't be able to support a spatial ring until Tier 15, and these are the next best thing. Most of the time, it's not the weight of what you are carrying that makes it awkward, it's the size of the items. At this point, each of you can carry a few hundred pounds, but good luck trying to hold that much crap.

"The price is an issue for all of them. The enchanted weapons are expensive despite being the most mundane of the three. Go check with the blacksmiths and enhancers for prices. The AIs are usually near three million credits, and the extra software is half that."

That was thirty Tier 4 mana stones, or three hundred Tier 3 mana stones.

"The spatial bags are also around the same price. Also, those prices are with the 50% off you get for being in the PlayPen. Bags being the exception and having a greater discount."

Matt blanched. Getting three hundred Tier 3 mana stones wasn't impossible in six months, but double that would require some good luck. He didn't think he had any more luck in the tank after surviving the fight to get Aster.

"So, that's all from me. The general store has the last two items and, no, I won't give you suggestions on what you should get. It's dependent on what you think you and your team needs. As well as luck." The last seemed to be tossed out as an afterthought.

The others quickly thanked Griff and quickly left.

Matt waited until they were out the door before he asked, "You said the AIs reserve mana but can eat into non-reserved mana if it was computing too much. Is there an AI that doesn't reserve mana?"

Griff looked at him with pursed lips before saying, "Yeah, there is, but it's the researcher's version. The normal AIs are all the same base but specialized. They reserve mana because they are hyper-efficient at their one task. The other software lets the AI do other things, but the core of the machine is built to do one of the tasks incredibly well. They'll never be as *efficient* as the others."

Seeing Matt open his mouth, Griff put up a hand and said, "It doesn't mean it won't be as good, just that it costs more mana."

With that, the older man packed his stuff up.

"I know what you are thinking and, yes, the researcher AI would be perfect for you. They eat dozens of mana per minute. Most researchers are pure mana cultivators, nearly 90% allocation, just so they can run the simulations and computations needed for their jobs."

Matt was shocked. How had Griff guessed why he couldn't use the normal AIs?

"Don't look so shocked. Take an acting class kid. Or play some poker. You show every thought on your face."

The Tier 15 shook his head. "I figured it out when I saw you with your skill active. One, you didn't, and still don't, have a veil up to hide your cultivation and mana pool. And two, I could feel the absurd amount of mana you were generating while it was active. Then, after the skill stopped, your mana generation plummeted. I can make some guesses."

Matt didn't know what to say. He was fearful Griff might do something but realized it was stupid when he thought of how much the man had done for him.

"I ugh—"

"Cut it. I don't care to look into it. You keep your secrets. I'd suggest you take the veil course as soon as possible, though."

Griff gave him a hard look. It worried Matt because he had no idea what the man might do.

"This is *not* a recommendation. I am not *legally* allowed to give recommendations during this class. But, if I had your mana problems, I would contact the manufacturer of the AIs. They have a location in almost every world for troubleshooting purposes."

Griff held up a finger. "They pay handsomely for high Tier cultivator's AI scans. That's how the new generations are made. They see how the older AIs process information, and they build better base models around that. The AIs grow with use, and everyone uses them differently after all.

"My AI is old. Old enough that it's two generations behind the current models. I have a DK model when the newest ones are DM models. The new models start out a bit better, but it's no substitute for time in the field and learning on its own, but it's a better starting point.

"Now, I know they love unique Talents that produce mana, and they pay handsomely for the privilege to test odd configurations of skills or Talents. That's where the best breakthroughs come from. The normal folks are good for testing baselines, but the odd Talents interacting with the AIs are how interesting advancements are made."

Griff shot him another hard look. "If I had a Talent that produced a lot of mana, I'd contact them and see if I could work out a deal."

"Won't they be able to know everything about someone if they get a scan of the AI in the future?" Matt couldn't let that happen at any cost.

"No, they scan the structure the AI becomes in your spirit, then run the AI through testing and benchmark the results. They don't get any personal information. They'd piss off far too many high-Tiered people if it came to light. And, well, that's a good way to end up dead.

"But I. Did. Not. Recommend. *Anything* to you." With a final hard look, Griff hurried out of the room.

TO BE CONTINUED IN

VOLUME 2